In Strange Gardens

and *Other Stories*

In Strange Gardens

and Other Stories

Peter Stamm

translated by Michael Hofmann

Other Press • New York

"Black Ice" was originally published as *Blitzeis*, © 1999 by Peter Stamm. First published in the German language by Arche Verlag AG, Zürich-Hamburg, 1999.

"In Strange Gardens" was originally published as *In Fremden Gärten*, © 2003 by Peter Stamm. First published in the German language by Arche Verlag AG, Zürich-Hamburg, 2003.

Translation copyright © 2006 Michael Hofmann

First softcover edition 2011
ISBN 978-1-59051-498-6

Production Editor: Robert D. Hack
Text design: Kaoru Tamura
This book was set in Sabon LT by Alpha Graphics, Pittsfield, NH.

Library of Congress Cataloging-in-Publication Data

Stamm, Peter, 1963-
    [Short stories. English. Selections]
    In strange gardens and other stories / Peter Stamm ; translated by Michael Hofmann.
        p. cm.
    Published in German in 2 collections: Blitzeis (1999) and In fremden Gärten (2003).
    ISBN 1-59051-169-7
    1. Stamm, Peter, 1963—Translations into English. I. Stamm, Peter, 1963- In fremden Gärten. English. II. Stamm, Peter, 1963- Blitzeis. English. III. Hofmann, Michael, 1957 Aug. 25- IV. Title.
    PT2681.T3234A2 2006
    833'.914—dc22   2005029502

TABLE OF CONTENTS

BLACK ICE

But I can't be talkin' of love, dear
I can't be talkin' of love.
If there be one thing I can't talk of
That one thing do be love.

—Esther Mathews

ICE LAKE

I had come home on the evening train from the French part of Switzerland. I was working in Neuchâtel at the time, but home was still my village in the Thurgau. I was just twenty.

There had been an accident somewhere, a fire, I don't remember what. At any rate, the train came from Geneva half an hour late, and it wasn't the normal express but a short train with old cars. It kept stopping in the middle of nowhere, and the passengers got into conversation with each other, and opened the windows. It was summer, vacation time. Outside, it smelled of hay, and once, when the train had stopped somewhere for quite some time and the country around was very quiet, we heard the screaking of cicadas.

It was almost midnight when I got to my village. The air was still warm, and I slung my jacket over my arm. My parents had already gone to bed. The house was dark, and I did nothing more than dump my carrier bag full of dirty clothes in the corridor. It didn't feel like a night for sleeping.

I found my friends standing outside the local, wondering what to do with themselves. The landlord had told them to go home, licensing hours were over. We talked out on the street for a while, till someone opened a window and shouted to us to shut up and go away. Then Urs's girlfriend Stefanie said: "Why don't we go up to Ice Lake and go for a swim? The water's really warm."

The others headed off, and I said I would just fetch my bike and catch up with them. I packed my trunks and towel, and then I set off after them. Ice Lake was in a valley between two villages. I was halfway there, when I ran into Urs heading the other way.

"Stefanie's got a flat," he called out to me. "I'm just going back for a puncture kit."

Shortly afterwards, I saw Stefanie sitting by the side of the road. I dismounted.

"Urs might be a while," I said. "I'll go with you, if you like."

We pushed our bikes slowly up the hill behind which the pond lay. I had never been especially keen on Stefanie, perhaps because they said she would try it on with anybody, perhaps because I was jealous because Urs never went anywhere without her. But now, alone with her for the first time, I seemed to get on with her okay, and we talked pretty easily about all sorts of things.

Stefanie had taken her final exams in the spring, and was working as a cashier in a supermarket until going on to college in the fall. She talked about shoplifters, and who in the village bought only sale items, and who bought condoms. We laughed all the way up the hill. When we got to the pond, we saw the others had all swum out already. We got undressed, and when I saw that Stefanie didn't have her swimsuit with her, I didn't put on my trunks either, and made as though that were quite natural. There wasn't a moon but there were loads of stars, and dim starlight on the hills and the pond.

Stefanie had jumped into the water, and was swimming in a different direction from our friends. I set off after her. The air was a bit cooler already and the grass was wet with dew, but the water was just as warm as it was by day. Only when I reached down with my feet and kicked hard did I stir up cooler water from underneath. When I had caught up to Stefanie, we swam side by side for a while, and she asked me if I had a girlfriend in Neuchâtel, and I said I didn't.

"Come on, we'll swim to the boathouse," she said.

We reached the boathouse, and looked back. We saw that the others were back on the shore by now, and had got a campfire going. We couldn't tell whether Urs had joined them yet or not. Stefanie climbed up onto the pier, and then onto the balcony, from where we had often dived into the water when we were kids. She lay on her back and told me to join her, she was feeling cold. I lay down next to her, but she said: "Come closer, that's no good."

We stayed on the balcony for a while. In the meantime the moon had come up, and it was so bright that our bodies cast shadows on the gray weathered wood. From the forest behind us we could hear sounds, but we didn't know what they were, and then someone was swimming toward the boathouse, and Urs's voice called out: "Stefanie, are you there?"

Stefanie put her finger to her lips, and pulled me back into the shadow of the tall rail. We heard Urs panting as he climbed out of the water, and pulled himself up on the rails. He had to be standing directly over us. I didn't dare look up, or stir.

"What are you doing there?" Urs was crouched on the balcony rail, looking down at us. His voice was quiet, surprised, not angry, and he was talking to me.

"We heard you coming," I said. "We were talking, and then we hid, to surprise you."

Now Urs looked over at the middle of the balcony, and I looked that way too, and the damp patch that my body and Stefanie's had made was as clear as if we were still there.

"What did you do that for?" asked Urs. Once again, he was addressing me, he seemed not to notice his girlfriend, who was crouching motionless in the shadow. Then he got up, and high above us on the rail he took a couple of steps, and with a sort of cry, a whoop, he leapt into the dark water. Even before the splash, I could hear a dull impact, and I jumped up and looked down.

Leaping off the balcony was dangerous. There were some poles stuck in the water that reached up to the surface;

when we were kids we knew where they were. Urs was floating on the water. His body had an odd white shimmer in the moonlight, and Stefanie, who was standing beside me now, said right away: "He's dead."

I carefully climbed down from the balcony onto the pier, grabbed Urs by an ankle, and pulled him toward me. Stefanie had jumped down from the balcony, and swum back to the others as fast as she could. I pulled Urs out of the water, and heaved him onto the little pier in front of the boathouse. He had a horrible wound on his head.

I think I mainly just sat next to him. Some time, a lot later, a policeman turned up and gave me a blanket, I hadn't realized how cold I was. The policeman took Stefanie and me back to the station, and we told them what had happened, but not what we had done on the balcony. They were very friendly, and when it was morning they even gave us a ride home. My parents were worried about me.

I saw Stefanie at Urs's funeral. The others were there too, but we didn't talk, not till later in the bar, and then not about what had happened that night. We drank beer, and someone, I can't remember who it was, said he wasn't sorry Stefanie had stopped coming. Ever since she'd started turning up, we hadn't had any proper conversations any more.

A few months later, I heard that Stefanie was pregnant. From then on, I started spending most of my weekends in Neuchâtel, and I even started doing my own laundry.

FLOTSAM

May God forgive the hands that fed
The false lights over the rocky head!
—John Greenleaf Whittier

I wasn't sure whether I'd called the right number or not. There was a snatch of classical music on the answering machine, and then the beep, and then the expectant silence of the recording. I called a second time. Once again, there was just music, and this time I left a message. Half an hour later, Lotta called me back. When we had gotten to know each other better, she told me about Joseph. He was the reason why she couldn't leave her voice on the tape. He musn't learn that she was back in the city.

Lotta was Finnish, and she lived in the West Village in Manhattan. I was looking for an apartment. An agency had given me Lotta's number.

"I sometimes have to rent the apartment," said Lotta, "when I don't have any work."

"And where do you live then?"

"Usually with friends," she said, "but this time I couldn't find anyone. Do you know of anywhere I can go?"

The apartment was big enough for two, so I offered to let her stay in it. She agreed right away.

"You must never pick up the phone," she said. "Always wait till you know who's calling. If you want to talk to me, call my name, and I'll switch off the answering machine."

"Were you there the first time I called?" I asked.

"Yes," she said.

Lotta lived on the fourth floor of an old building on 11th Street. Everything in the apartment was black, the furniture, the sheets, the rugs. A few withered cactuses stood on the little wrought iron balcony that opened out onto the yard. On the table by Lotta's bed, and the glass-topped table that had the answering machine on it, there were dusty shells and twigs of coral. The few lamps had red and green bulbs in them, which made the rooms look odd at night, as if they were under water.

When I came to inspect the apartment, Lotta had answered the door in pajamas, even though it was midday. After showing me round the place, she went straight back to bed. I asked her if she was ill, but she shook her head and said, no, she just liked sleeping.

After I moved in, I never knew her to get up before midday, and usually she went to bed before me as well. She read a lot, and she drank coffee, but I rarely saw her eat anything. She seemed to live off coffee and chocolate. "You should have a healthier diet," I said, "then you wouldn't be so tired."

"But I like sleeping," she said, and smiled.

There was a black kitten living with us too. Lotta had been given it, and she called it Romeo. Later, she learned that Romeo was a girl, but the name stuck anyway.

It was October. I was meeting a couple of old friends, Werner and Graham, who were working for a bank. I suggested we go to the shore for a long weekend. Graham said we could take his car, and I asked Lotta to come along. We set off on a Friday morning. We wanted to go to Block Island, which is a little island about a hundred miles east of Manhattan.

We made our first stop in Queens. We were late setting out, and already hungry. We bought hotdogs from a stand on the road. Lotta just drank coffee. At a crossroads a little way ahead of us was a black man, who was standing beside a cardboard box full of vacuum-packed meat. Whenever the lights turned red, he would go from car to car and try to interest the people in the meat. When he caught sight of us he came running up, with one of the packages in his hand. We stopped and talked to him for a while. He spoke better French than English, and we asked him what he was doing in Queens. He didn't mind our kidding around with him; probably he was hoping we would buy something from him. Even as we drove off, he was still smiling, waving his packages at us, and calling out something after us that we couldn't understand.

We got onto the island on the last ferry of the day. We had left the car in an almost deserted carpark on the mainland. The crossing took two hours, and even though it was cold, Werner spent the whole time outside, leaning on the railing. The rest of us sat in the cafeteria. The ship was almost empty.

Right next to the port on the island there was a big, crumbling turn-of-the-century hotel. Not far away was a simple B and B in a shiny, white-painted clapboard house. Lotta and I shared a room—it seemed the natural thing to do.

There was a near gale blowing in off the sea. All the same, we thought we'd take a walk before supper. There was a gray wooden boardwalk going along the shore. Once outside the village, it suddenly stopped, and we had to trudge on through sand.

Werner and I were walking together. He was very quiet. Graham and Lotta had taken off their shoes, and were looking for shells nearer the tide line. Before long, they had dropped back. Only occasionally we heard a shout or Lotta's high-pitched laugh through the roar of the surf.

After we'd walked along a while, Werner and I sat down on the sand to wait for the others. We could see their silhouettes black against the glinting water.

"What are those two doing down there?" I asked.

"Picking up shells," said Werner placidly. "We've gone a long way."

I clambered up onto a dune to look back. Sand leaked into my shoes, and I took them off. The village was a long way away. Some of the houses already had lights on. When I came back down, Werner had got up and walked down to the water. Lotta and Graham were sitting in the shelter of a dune. They had put their shoes back on. I sat down beside them and we looked silently out to sea, and watched Werner throwing rocks or shells into the water. The wind blew up little tornadoes of sand along the beach.

"I'm cold," said Lotta.

On the way back, I walked with Lotta and helped her carry some of the shells she'd picked up. I had knotted together my shoelaces, and my shoes were dangling over my shoulder. The sand felt chilly underfoot. Graham was walking on ahead, Werner was following us at a distance.

"I like Graham," said Lotta.

"They work in a bank," I said, "him and Werner. But they're okay."

"How old is he?"

"We're all the same age as each other. We went to school together."

Lotta talked about Finland. She had grown up on a farm, north of Helsinki. Her father had bred bulls. Lotta had left home early, and gone first to Berlin, then London, then Florence. Finally, four or five years ago, she had turned up in New York.

"Last Christmas I visited my parents. For the first time in years. My father's not well. At first, my plan was to stay with them, but I came back in May." She hesitated. "I suppose I only went away on account of Joseph."

"What happened with Joseph? Were you an item?"

Lotta shrugged her shoulders. "It's a long story. I'll save it for some other time."

As we were approaching the village, we turned around to look for Werner. He was a long way back, and was walking slowly down by the water's edge. When he saw us waiting for him, he waved and speeded up a bit.

We had supper in a little fish restaurant. Lotta said she was a vegetarian, but Graham reckoned she was allowed to eat fish anyway. We paid for her, and she ate whatever the rest of us ate, but she didn't drink any wine.

After Lotta had been silent a while, Graham and I sometimes lapsed into our native tongue. Werner didn't speak, and it didn't seem to bother Lotta either way. She ate slowly and with concentration, as if she had to think about every move and every bite. She noticed me watching her and smiled, and only went on eating when I'd stopped looking at her.

At night, Lotta wore pink pajamas with appliquéd teddy bears. She had short blond hair. She was certainly over thirty, but she seemed like a little kid. She lay on her back, and had pulled the covers up to her chin. I rested my head on my hands, and looked at her.

"Do you think you're going to stay in New York?" I asked.

"No," said Lotta, "I don't like the climate."

"Is Finland any better?" I asked.

"At home I was always cold. I want to go to Trinidad. I've got a lot of friends there."

"You've got a lot of friends, period."

"Yes," said Lotta.

"Well, you've got some friends in Switzerland now."

"I'd like to have a little shop in Trinidad," she said. "Cosmetics, films, aspirin . . . things imported from here. You can't get that kind of thing over there. Or else it's very expensive."

"Do they speak English on Trinidad?" I asked.

"I think so. My friends speak English . . . well, and it's always warm."

On the road below, a car drove past. Its headlights sliced through the blinds, swung across the room, up onto the ceiling, and suddenly went out, just over our bed.

"You have a lot of freedom," I said. But Lotta was already asleep.

We met Werner and Graham at breakfast.

"Did you sleep well?" asked Graham with a grin.

"I like to be able to hear the ocean from bed," I said.

"I was very tired," said Lotta.

Werner ate in silence.

It started raining in the morning, and we went to the local museum. It was housed in a little white barn. There's not much to report on the history of Block Island. Some time it was discovered by a Dutchman by the name of Block.

Some settlers crossed from the mainland. Not too much happened after that.

The old fellow who ran the museum told us about the many ships that had run aground on the reefs in front of the island. The locals had lived from flotsam and jetsam more than they had ever done from fishing.

"People say they lured the ships ashore with false lights," said the man, and laughed. Nowadays the island was living off tourism. In summer, every ferry was full of summerfolk, and a lot of wealthy New York people kept summerhouses there. For a while it had been quite the thing to have a house on Block Island. But today a lot of those people flew to the Caribbean.

"Things have gotten quieter here," said the man, "but we can't complain. Ships no longer come to grief here, but all kinds of things still get washed ashore."

Lotta asked him whether he was a fisherman.

"I used to be a realtor," he said. "You can't imagine the kind of things that get washed up here."

He laughed, I didn't know why.

Then we went down to the beach again. Lotta started looking for shells again, we others sat down and smoked. Graham took a shard of crab's claw and dug a hole with it in the fine sand, which grew waterlogged just below the surface.

"Well," I said, "what did I tell you? She's quite nice, don't you think?"

Werner didn't say anything. Graham laughed. "What are we going to be able to say about her, we don't get to sleep in the same bed with her."

"The sound of that: sleep in the same bed with. Why don't you say what you're really thinking."

"It's my turn tonight," said Graham with a grin, "and tomorrow it's Werner's. But he doesn't go in for that kind of thing."

I told him he was being an idiot, and Werner said: "Come on, stop it." He stood up and walked off, down to the sea. Lotta came back, with her hands full of shells. She sat down in the sand next to us, spread out her bounty, and began slowly wiping each shell with her fingers. Graham picked up a spiral shell from between Lotta's legs, and examined it for a long time.

"Strange, what nature throws up," he said, and laughed. "What was it the man said? You can't imagine what washes up here."

The noon ferry brought a few more tourists ashore, but they quickly dispersed in various directions, and before long the village was deserted again. We ate on the terrace of a coffee shop.

"What now?" I asked.

"I'm tired," said Lotta. "I think I'll go and lie down for an hour."

Graham set off to look for a newspaper, and Werner said he was going down to the sea. I strolled back to the hotel with Lotta.

The beds in our room had been made up, and the window was wide open. Lotta shut it, and pulled down the blinds. She lay down. I sat down on the floor and leaned against the bed.

"I wonder how poor little Romeo's doing," said Lotta. "I do miss him terribly."

"I'm sure he's fine."

"Don't you want to lie down?"

"I'm not tired."

"I can always sleep," said Lotta.

In the late afternoon, we rented some bicycles to go and view the Palatine graves on the south of the island. That's where sixteen Dutchmen who survived the famous wreck of the Palatine are supposed to be buried.

"Why are they buried if they survived?" asked Lotta.

"Buried alive," said Graham.

Werner laughed.

"It was in the eighteenth century," I said.

"But why were they buried together then?" asked Lotta. "Just because they were on the same ship?"

"Perhaps because they were rescued together," I suggested. "They must have bonded."

We found a crumbly signpost somewhere, but we never found the graves. We saw a man in a meadow. He didn't know where the graves were either. He had never even heard of them. Disappointed, we turned back.

"I don't care," said Lotta, "I don't like graveyards anyway."

We were riding into the wind now, and only reached the hotel after dark. We drank a beer. Lotta called her neighbor, to see if her cat was okay.

"Everything's fine," she said, coming back.

"It's Werner's thirtieth birthday next week," I said to Lotta. "We should have a party for him."

"That makes you a Libra," she said. "Joseph was a Libra as well."

"What Joseph?" Graham asked. "As in Joseph and Mary?"

"As in Joseph and Lotta, more like," I said.

"A friend," said Lotta.

"Libra," muttered Graham, and leafed through his newspaper. Then he read out: "You are facing a decision, and should be realistic about it. It shouldn't be difficult for you to strike up new acquaintances. Happy hours lie ahead."

"That's a good horoscope," said Lotta.

Werner laughed. It was an odd, mocking laugh. Graham and I laughed along, but Lotta merely smiled, and laid her hand on Werner's arm.

"It's all right," she said. "Come on, let's go for a walk."

They got up, and we arranged to meet up in an hour in the fish restaurant where we'd gone the night before. Werner walked upright and stiff like an invalid. He looked as though he wasn't moving at all. Lotta pushed her arm through his. She seemed to be driving him onward, down toward the beach.

"So," said Graham, after we'd been silent for a long time, "what's she like then?"

"What do you mean?"

"Don't play the innocent. What else did you bring her along for?"

"She's a strange woman," I said. "Don't you think so?"

Graham grinned. "A woman's a woman."

"No," I said, "I like her. I like being with her."

"Which one of the three of us do you think she likes best?" asked Graham.

"I think you're the one who's desperate to be liked by her."

"Ach, give over. I like it that she's always so tired. They're good in bed. I know the sort."

"Listen, guy, you should remember you're married."

"I'm on vacation. Do you think I've come to look for seashells?"

"What does Werner say?" I asked.

"Nothing. Werner says absolutely nothing. I've never known him so quiet. He's like a fish."

We finished our beer. Graham said he needed to phone, and I sat down in an armchair in the lobby of the hotel and started flicking through the *Fisherman's Quarterly*.

Lotta didn't come to supper. She was tired, explained Werner as he came to the table alone. He was as quiet as ever during the meal, but the earnestness of the past few days was gone, and he sometimes put down his knife and fork and smiled quietly to himself.

"Are we in love then?" asked Graham mockingly.

"No," said Werner curtly but not angrily. And he calmly went on eating. Over coffee he said we ought to go and look at the chalk cliffs on the south of the island tomorrow.

"They must be somewhere near the Palatine graves then," I said. "I don't know about cycling all the way down there again . . ."

Graham had no desire to cross the island again.

"Just on account of a few chalk cliffs. There are chalk cliffs all over Europe. In England, in Brittany, in Ireland, all over."

But Werner wouldn't be deterred, and merely said: "Well, you don't have to come if you don't want."

At midnight Werner went off to bed. Graham and I sat around for a long time after. We had had quite a bit to drink. Graham said his wife had moved out. She was now living with her English tutor.

"She didn't get a work permit," he said. "Then she wanted a baby, but that didn't work. She was bored."

I felt sorry for Graham. Then I suddenly realized that I disliked him. I said I was tired and was going to bed. He ordered two more beers, but I got up and went anyway.

Lotta seemed to be fast asleep when I walked into the room. Her breathing was loud and irregular. I got undressed, opened the window a crack, and lay down beside her. I listened to her breathing and to the roar of the sea, but I soon fell asleep, and only woke up when I heard someone banging on the door. I saw right away that Lotta wasn't there, but I didn't think anything of it. It was mid-morning. Graham was standing outside the door.

"Werner's gone," he said.

"Lotta is too," I said. "Maybe they're having breakfast."

"No," said Graham, "I've been downstairs and looked."

We ate our own breakfast.

"Perhaps they went down to the sea," I suggested, "or to look at the cliffs."

"Well, one thing for sure, they haven't taken their bicycles," said Graham, "and it must be two hours on foot."

We both felt irritated. When Werner and Lotta weren't back by lunchtime, we took the bicycles and rode south. But there were two roads, and if Werner and Lotta were walking, there was no knowing which one they would have taken. A couple of hours later, we were back in the bed and breakfast.

"They're going to get such a tongue-lashing when they get back," said Graham.

The woman at the front desk wanted to see us. She said we needed to clear out our rooms. Our friends had left while we were gone. They had left a note. She passed me a piece of paper where Lotta had written we weren't to worry, and should drive home without them. She and Werner would make their own way back.

"I sensed your Finn wasn't too picky," said Graham, "but taking off with Werner . . ."

"I can't understand why they left," I said. "We had nice times together."

"Werner won," said Graham. "Simple as that."

He was grinning, but he couldn't mask his fury.

"She's her own person," I said, "she's free to go with anyone she likes."

There was just enough time to pack our things before the next ferry departed for the mainland.

The crossing was cold and windy. By the time we got to the car the entire sky had clouded over, and shortly after we drove off it started raining. We barely talked. Graham was livid, and drove much too fast. He was going back to Switzerland, he said, he had had it with America. His wife would have to go back with him, like it or not. After all, she was still dependent on him for money.

Outside Bridgeport we stopped for gas, and I tried calling Werner and then Lotta. But Werner wasn't there, and Lotta's answering machine played only music, as though nothing had happened. After the signal I yelled out: "Lotta, are you there? Lotta!"

I imagined my voice echoing through the empty apartment, felt stupid, and hung up.

We drove through the Bronx to Queens, where Graham lived. I went up with him. His place was a mess, dirty plates in the kitchen. While Graham played back phone messages, I made coffee. There was an agitated voice on the tape, but I couldn't hear much over the boiling water. When I walked into the sitting room, Graham was sitting slumped on the sofa, with the phone pressed to his ear. I poured the coffee. Graham said yes once or twice, and then thank you, and then he hung up.

"Werner's killed himself," he said. "He wrote a farewell note before we set out on Friday. That was his landlady I was talking to. She has a key to his place and was looking around it yesterday. It was because it was raining, she said, and she wanted to check that all the windows were closed."

He told me the whole, utterly irrelevant story as if he was terrified of silence.

"The note was on the kitchen table. The woman is Hungarian, she knows a bit of German, and she understood the gist of it. But she didn't know where we were going. She found my number next to the phone. She called a couple of other people as well."

"But Lotta," I said, "surely she didn't . . . After all, she wrote that we weren't to worry about her. They were going to make their own way home . . ."

Graham shrugged his shoulders.

"Do you think he wanted to . . . do you think he jumped off the cliff?" I asked. "I don't think he's capable of that. He's not a romantic."

"Well, I'm sure he didn't have a gun," said Graham.

"What are we going to do?" I asked.

"I don't know," he said. "It's too early to go to the police."

He wanted to give me a ride into the city, but I said he ought to stay by the phone. I didn't feel like talking, I wanted to be alone. The two cups of coffee sat on the table, untouched.

The subway station was almost deserted. I had to wait fifteen minutes for a train. As we approached Manhattan, it gradually filled up. I got out one station before my usual stop, and walked the last few blocks. It wasn't raining any more, but the streets were still wet. I bought a beer and a sandwich at a convenience store.

As I opened the front door of the apartment, I could hear Lotta's voice. The answering machine was on, and was recording. At first I wanted to pick up the receiver and speak to her, but then I didn't and just listened. "The furniture all belongs to Joseph. And Romeo . . . Robert, please will you look after Romeo. He's so little. Promise me you won't let anything happen to him. You can stay in the apartment too. You'll just have to sort it out with Joseph. Tell him you've paid the agency fees." There was silence for a moment.

"I think that's everything. Be well, and don't be mad at us. Bye Graham, bye Robert."

She whispered: "Do you want to say anything else?"

I heard Werner clearly say no. Then there was a click, and the connection was broken. I pictured Lotta turning to face Werner, in some bus stop or restaurant, and he smiling, and the two of them going off together and disappearing. I thought I'd missed my last chance to speak to her, or at least to say goodbye.

I rewound the tape and listened to it from the beginning.

"You have . . . TWO messages," said the synthetic voice. Then I heard my voice: "Lotta, are you there? Lotta!" I sounded nervous and angry, worried. There were a couple of clicks, and then Lotta spoke: "Hello, is anyone home? Hello, Robert, hello!" She sighed, and then she said: "Ah well, then you're still on your way back. Doesn't matter. I'm calling from a restaurant. We're in . . . where are we?"

I could hear them whispering.

"We're near Philadelphia. I'm with Werner. We're traveling together. Originally, Werner was going to . . . well, he left a note in his apartment. But he's changed his mind. We're going traveling together. He's fixed everything. You'll understand when you see the note. I don't have much that needs taking care of. Robert? If you get this, will you call Joseph. He knows about everything. You'll find his number on the list next to the phone. I came back to the apartment quickly to pick up a few things. I don't need any more. The furniture belongs to Joseph . . ."

I stopped the tape, and called Graham. We didn't talk for long. When I got myself a beer, Romeo walked into the kitchen. There was some milk in the fridge. "Do you know where your children are" it said on the package, and underneath was a picture and a short description of a missing child.

The milk had gone bad, and I poured it away. In one of the cupboards there was a can of cat food. I turned on the TV, lay down on the sofa, and drank my beer.

A few days later I called Joseph, and asked if I could meet him. I said I was a friend of Lotta's. He cleared his throat and said we could meet at his restaurant, which was on the corner of Vandam and Houston.

I went there the next morning. The place was dark and empty. There was one short, stout man sitting reading the paper at a table at the back. He was balding, and fifty. He stood up as I approached the table, and we shook hands.

"You must be Robert. I'm pleased to meet you. I'm Joseph. What's Lotta up to?"

He asked me to sit down, and went behind the bar to get me a coffee.

"I'm Lotta's subtenant," I said.

"So she's back from Finland. I thought she might be."

"She's disappeared," I said.

He laughed. "Milk and sugar? She does have a habit of disappearing."

"Black, please," I said. "She disappeared with a friend of mine. No idea where."

Joseph sat down opposite. "The building is mine," he said. "Lotta didn't pay any rent. Don't look at me that way. It's not as though I'm married."

"There was nothing between us," I said. "We just shared the apartment."

"I'm not surprised," said Joseph, and drank his coffee. "Lotta's one of those wandering scrounging types. New York's full of them. They take whatever they can get, and give you nothing back."

"I always wanted to live the way she does," I said. "I like her. She's nice."

"Sure. Why do you think I let her live in the place for free?"

I smiled, and then he smiled too.

"How long do you want to keep the apartment for?"

"Three weeks still. I've paid the rent. I've got a receipt here . . ."

"That's fine. You can stay as long as you like."

"What about Lotta's things?" I asked. "She said she wouldn't be needing them any more."

"Just leave everything the way it is," he said. "She'll be back one day."

IN THE OUTER SUBURBS

I'd spent Christmas Eve with friends. They'd uncorked some champagne in the afternoon, and I'd gone home early because I was drunk and I had a headache. I was living in a small studio apartment in West Queens. In the morning I was awakened by the phone. It was my parents calling from Switzerland, to wish me a merry Christmas. It wasn't a long conversation, we didn't know what else to say to each other. It was raining outside. I made myself some coffee, and read.

In the afternoon I went for a walk. For the first time since I'd been there, I headed out of town, toward the outer suburbs. I hit Queens Boulevard, and followed it east. It was a wide straight road, cutting through precincts that didn't change much or at all. Sometimes it was shops, and I had a sense of being in some sort of conurbation, and then I found myself in residential districts of tenements or small, squalid row houses. I crossed a bridge over an old, overgrown set of rails. Then there was an enclosed patch of waste ground, full of trash and rubble, and an enormous crossroads with no lights and no traffic. After that I came to another bunch of shops and a cross-street that had a subway stop on top of it, like a roof. The Christmas decorations in the store-fronts and the tinsel hanging over the streets, disarrayed by rain and wind, looked like ancient remnants.

The rain had let up, and I stopped on the corner to light a cigarette. I wasn't sure whether to go on or not. Then a young woman came up to me, and asked for a light. She said it was her birthday. If I had twenty dollars on me, we could buy a few things and have ourselves a little party.

"I'm sorry," I said, "I haven't got it on me."

She said that didn't matter, I was to wait here for her anyway. She was going shopping, and would be back.

"Funny, it being your birthday on Christmas Day."

"Yes," she said, as though it had never occurred to her, "I suppose you're right."

She went off down the street, and I knew she wouldn't be back. I knew it wasn't her birthday either, but I would still have gone with her if I'd had the money. I finished my cigarette, and lit another. Then I started back. There was a bar across the street. I went in and asked for a beer.

"Are you French?" asked the man next to me. "I'm Dylan." As in the great poet Dylan Thomas, he said, *light breaks where no sun shines* . . .

"Did you ever," Dylan asked me, "read a love poem from a woman to a man?"

"No," I said, "I don't read poetry."

"I tell you, you're making a mistake there. You'll find everything in poetry. Everything."

He got up and went down a short flight of stairs to the rest room. When he came back, he stood next to me, put his arm round me, and said: "There aren't any! Women don't love men, believe me."

The barman gave me a signal I didn't understand. Dylan pulled a tattered volume from his pocket and held it over our heads.

"Immortal Poems of the English Language," he said. "It's my Bible."

There were dirty little scraps of paper stuck in between many of the pages. Dylan opened the book at a certain place.

"Now, listen to the way women love men," he said, and he read out: "Mrs. Elizabeth Barrett Browning: How do I love thee? Let me count the ways . . . Not one word about him. All Mrs. Browning does is say how much she loves him, how magnificent her feelings for him are. Here's another one . . ."

An old man next to me whispered: "He's always doing that." And he made the same signal as the barman before him. I started to get it, but I was already feeling a bit drunk, and I didn't want to go just yet. I just smiled, and turned to face Dylan who had turned to another poem.

"Miss Bronte," he said, "same story! Cold in the earth, and the deep snow piled above thee! Far, far removed . . . That's how it starts, and then it's all about her pain. Nothing about the guy. Or this . . . Mrs. Rossetti: My heart is like a singing bird . . . My heart is like an apple-tree . . . And so on, till the last line, which goes: Because my love is come to me. Do you call that love? Is that the way a person in love would write? Only someone in love with herself."

He put the book away, and put his short arm around me again.

"You know, my friend, there's no such thing as a woman's love. They love us like children, or the way the creator might love the thing he's created. But as little as we find peace with God do we find peace with women."

"Does that make God a woman?" I asked.

"Of course," said Dylan, "and Jesus is Her daughter."

"And you're his sister," said the barman.

"I don't like women with beards," said the old fellow on the other side of me.

We fell silent.

"Homosexuals will all go to Hell," said the old man.

"I'm not going to get involved on that level," said Dylan angrily, and moved closer to me, as if seeking protection. "The two of us were talking about poetry. This young man here doesn't have the prejudices of you two clowns."

"The next round's on the house," said the barman, and he put a cassette of Christmas tunes on the stereo behind him.

"God rest ye, merry gentlemen," sang Harry Belafonte.

"Yo," went a young man at one of the tables, "he misadeh misadeeho . . ."

The barman set our beers down on the bar in front of us. I was pretty drunk by now. I raised my glass, and said: "To poetry!"

"Well, don't say I didn't warn you," said the old man.

"Now read the poems that men have written for women," said Dylan, and he recited from memory: "She is as in a field a silken tent, at midday when a sunny summer breeze has dried the dew . . ."

Overcome, he stopped, looked down at the dirty floor, and sadly shook his head.

"Women call themselves romantics, as if they would call themselves American," he said. "They love it when you say you're beautiful, your eyes shine like the sun, your lips are red as coral, your breasts are white as snow. They think they're romantic because they like to be adored by men."

I wanted to contradict, but he said: "I just want to open your eyes. Don't let women make a fool of you. They'll tempt you with their spare flesh. And once you've bitten, they'll break your head open and eat you up."

I laughed.

"You remind me of someone," said Dylan.

"Some friend of yours?" I asked.

"A very good friend. He's dead now."

I went to the rest room.

"I've got no money left for the bus now," I said.

"I'll take you home," said Dylan.

I thought it must be dark by now, but as we stepped out of the bar, it was a fine afternoon. The rain had stopped.

There were still clouds in the sky. But the low sun shone through underneath them. The houses and trees and cars glistened and projected long shadows. Dylan had his car parked on Queens Boulevard. He turned into a sidestreet.

"That's not my way home," I said. "You're going the wrong way."

Dylan laughed. "Are you scared of me?" he asked.

I didn't say anything.

"I'm just turning the car around," he said. "Are you that scared of women too?"

"I don't know . . . I guess not."

We drove back toward Manhattan in silence. I hadn't walked nearly as far as I thought.

"Here," I said, "I'd like to walk the last bit."

I got out, and walked around the car. Dylan had wound down the window and held out his hand.

"Thanks for the ride," I said, "and thanks for the beer."

Dylan wouldn't let go my hand till I looked into his eyes. Then he said: "Thanks for a pleasant afternoon."

As I crossed the street, he called after me: "And Merry Christmas."

EVERYONE'S RIGHT

> *And we lie here, our orient peace awaking*
> *No echo, and no shadow, and no reflection.*
> —Henry Reed

I could see Monika's yellow rain jacket through the trees. I had put on water for coffee when she called me. The forest was dense here, and the ground was covered with boughs and twigs that snapped underfoot. It was hard going, and after just a few steps my pants and my hands were filthy with moss and algae that covered everything with their slime.

"Quiet," said Monika softly, as I approached. Then I saw that Michael was curled up on the ground in front of her.

"What's the matter with him?" I asked, once I heard his noisy breathing.

"When he caught sight of me he ran off, and then he fell," said Monika. She knelt down, and shook Michael gently. "What happened? Where's Sandra?"

"I lost my shoe," he said, panting. "I can't find it anywhere."

"Where's Sandra?" asked Monika.

"Gone to get help."

It was only by chance that I had wound up in Sweden at all. Monika had recently broken up with her boyfriend, and since the canoe tour had already been booked, she asked me whether I'd like to go with her. I'd been in love with Monika back in high school, but there was one terrible night when she told me she wasn't in love with me. We had stayed friends, and I'd gone on hoping for a while, till one day she told me she had a lover. All that happened years ago.

We had run into Sandra and Michael on the train. They were both wearing purple fleeces and trousers with loads of pockets. Sandra said this was her fifth visit to Sweden, she had worked in the travel business, she loved the north, her car had been broken open and robbed once in Goteborg. She spoke Swedish place names as if she had mastered the language. When Monika asked her, she said no, unfortunately not, she just spoke German, French, Italian, and, of course, English. She said her name was Sandra, and her husband's was Michael.

"My husband's name is Michael," she said. "We're on our honeymoon."

Michael didn't say anything. He didn't even seem to be listening, and just stared out into the forest. Only once, when a heron flew up from close to the tracks, and cleared the treetops with a few lazy wingstrokes, did he say: "Sandra, look."

"This will be our last vacation for some time," said Sandra. "We're having a baby in six months. Isn't that right, Michael?"

Michael was staring out of the window again, and Sandra repeated: "Isn't that right, Michael?"

"Yes," he said eventually.

"You seem to be over the moon about it," said Monika, with an exaggeratedly warm smile.

"It seems such a miracle to me," said Sandra, "to feel a new life stirring within me."

"The real miracle will be when the life starts stirring on its own," said Monika tartly.

"Don't you want children?" asked Sandra, turning to me.

"Children aren't compatible with the interior design of our apartment," said Monika quickly.

The campsite was on the edge of a small town, between an automobile factory and the big lake. When we went to the store to buy provisions, we ran into Sandra and Michael again. Sandra said we had to buy mosquito repellent, and only Swedish mosquito repellent worked on Swedish mosquitoes.

"Have you vino?" an Austrian woman was asking at the checkout ahead of us. The checkout clerk shook her head, and Sandra told the woman about the Swedish laws governing the sale of alcohol.

"I can't stand that woman," Monika whispered in my ear. In the evening, as we were heading for the pizza joint next to the campsite, we saw Sandra and Michael crouching in front of their tent, cooking.

"We're having a proper adventure vacation," Sandra called out. "The pizza place is no good, and it's expensive."

Michael didn't say anything. It was true, the pizzas weren't very good, and they were really expensive. But Monika did imitations of Sandra all through supper, and we spent a fun evening.

"I can have much more of a laugh with you than I could with Stefan," she said.

"Is that why you split up?"

"No," said Monika. "He wanted to have a baby."

"And you?"

"He just wanted it because he was scared. All his friends were having babies. He was probably afraid everything would carry on in the same way. And that he would get old. All that. That's what he said."

"And you?" I asked again.

"Well, in the end, you're on your own anyway," said Monika.

"Don't you want a baby?"

"No. I want to get through life alone. Even if it means growing old on my own."

Monika said ideally she would have gone on the canoeing tour on her own as well. But then she had read that at some points you had to carry the boat across land for a little ways, and she didn't think she could do that. And so she'd asked me to come.

"So I'm here as your bearer?"

"No. You know what you mean to me. You're my oldest friend, and that's more than the greatest lover."

When we returned past Sandra and Michael's tent, we couldn't see them anymore. But from inside the tent we could hear Sandra moaning: "Oh, yes! Oh, give it to me! Oh, that's so good!"

Monika coughed and in a disguised voice called out something that might sound like Swedish. There was silence right away.

"I'm going for a shower," Monika said when we'd got to our tent. "Last showers before the highway."

By the time she was back, I was already in my sleeping bag.

"Turn away," she ordered. She undressed, and I smelled the fresh smell of soap. She clicked off the flashlight. We lay side by side, silently. Then Monika asked me: "Do you yell like that each time you sleep with a woman?"

"No," I said.

"Glad to hear it," said Monika. "Good night."

The next morning, when we went down to the canoe rental place, Michael and Sandra were already there. Sandra was talking about universal rights. Everyone was entitled to walk in the forest, and to go on the river, and pick mushrooms and firewood for his own personal use.

She said, basically you were allowed to live in the forest. Just like the animals, free, without money. To live off roots and berries, and whatever the forest would provide. Off the fruits of nature, was what she said.

"Hunger, cold, and disease," said Monika, "those are the fruits of nature."

Michael stood there silently. Then a canoe rental person came along, and we loaded the canoes onto an old bus, and drove to the starting point of our tour. The road led further and further into the forest. Our driver drove fast, and sometimes he jerked the steering wheel to the side, to avoid a pothole in the unmade road. And then he would laugh. Now it was Sandra who was very quiet, except once I heard her say: "I'm not going to be sick. It's just a matter of will power."

Sandra and Michael seemed to get their boat ready to go in no time at all. They paddled off, while the driver was still explaining the use of the camping stove to us, and how to tie the most important knot. We were to keep our life vests on at all times, and keep our baggage tied on, in case we should capsize. Then, before we had the canoe in the water, he had turned the bus, and vanished into the forest.

After a few hours I felt exhausted from the unfamiliar exercise, from the heat of the midday sun, and from the long journey the day before. But I didn't say anything, and paddled on in silence. Eventually I forgot the soreness in my arms, my strokes became calmer and more rhythmic, and we made steadier progress. I had the sense that my body had detached itself from my head, and was working automatically.

Then, all at once, it was late, and we were surprised that the sun was still so high in the sky. At eleven at night, you could still read a newspaper here out of doors, Sandra had told us in the train, but when we finally found a place to pitch our tent, we merely pitched it and made our supper.

"Ideally, I'd never stop," said Monika, "just keep going down the river, night and day."

"It would be nice not to know where we were going," I said.

"You never know where you're going anyway."

The following days all resembled each other. We got up late, made coffee, set out. Sometimes we swam in the river, or lay around on the grass during the midday heat. One sunny afternoon, we moored on a tiny island in the middle of a lake. We had something to eat. I had meant to read, but I was already too tired. I turned onto my back, and closed my eyes. The sun was bright, and I saw colorful whirling shapes in orange and light green that spun in circles. I fell asleep.

When I opened my eyes, the sky above me looked almost black. My mouth was dry, and my body felt warm and heavy. It took me a while to come round. With an effort I turned onto my side. Monika wasn't there, and I stood up and crossed the little patch of grass to the place where we'd fixed the boat. Monika's clothes lay on the grass. I looked out onto the lake, and saw her some way off.

"Come on in," she shouted, swimming back toward me, "the water's lovely."

"That sounds like a film," I said. "The water's lovely. People only say that in films."

"But it really is lovely."

"Funny, you can't even describe it."

"It's true," she said, "I can't describe it. Is that silly? But I really can't."

She emerged from the water. I had never seen her so nearly naked. Her hair was plastered against her head, and the water dribbled out of her bathing suit.

"Do you know that I used to be hopelessly in love with you?" I said. "You broke my heart. I thought you were the woman of my life."

"When was that?" asked Monika, shaking the water out of her hair.

"When you told me you didn't love me."

"Did I say that?" Suddenly she started laughing. "Oh, if only you could see your face. I remember. It was after our class trip. I was in love with Leo then, but he didn't like me."

"When was the first time you slept with a man?" I asked. I had sat down in the grass, and was looking at her. Monika turned her back to me, and pulled off her bathing suit. Then she dried herself with her towel, and got dressed. "I was seventeen," she said, and turned to face me again, "it was with a friend of my brother's. He was a lot older. Maybe ten years or so. You were all so childish then with your talk of undying love and God and the meaning of life. I just wanted to see what it felt like."

"That's all I wanted too."

"Nonsense," said Monika, "you were in love, you just said so."

We were now paddling through forested country, but we started looking at it more closely, and noticing that the landscape kept changing, and the colors and the water. The water was black or blue or dark green, and sometimes our canoe slipped through patches of water-lilies or through beds of reeds. When there was a wind, we kept inshore. In the evenings, we tried to tally up the days, and looked at the map to see how far we'd come. We soon lost all sense of time.

We hadn't seen another human being for days when we saw a canoe on the bank. Then we saw Sandra and Michael who were lying naked on the grass. I hoped they wouldn't see us, but they seemed to hear us, and looked up. They didn't wave, and we pretended we hadn't seen them.

"Lying there like animals," said Monika. "With her, I always have the feeling she's trying to prove something."

"Because she's having a baby?"

"No, it's not that," said Monika. "Haven't you ever seen children where you can just tell they're going to turn into idiots just like their parents? Even quite small children."

I thought I wouldn't mind lying naked with Monika in the grass, and I said so.

"Like an animal," said Monika. "I couldn't do that. I'd be scared."

"There's no one around."

"That would be why. There has to be some distinction."

"I mean just because we've known each other for so long," I said. "I wouldn't feel ashamed in front of you."

"I always wanted to be different from my parents. Even though I like my parents. But I don't want to be just a copy of them. It would be awful if everything just carried on being exactly the same." She hesitated. Then she said with a laugh: "And why would you feel ashamed anyway?"

When I looked back after a while, I saw Sandra and Michael sitting in their canoe, and coming after us. They were paddling as fast as they could, and shortly after, when they passed us without a word, I could hear their panting. They were dressed now, in swimsuits and T-shirts. Automatically, I started paddling faster, but Monika said, "Oh, don't. I don't feel like racing."

"But I don't want to have anybody in front of me," I said. "Do you think they knew it was you, at the campsite?"

"I don't care," said Monika. "Fuck them too."

The next afternoon we went swimming again. The water was cold, and we soon returned to the shore.

"They were here too," said Monika, picking up a chocolate wrapper that was lying on the sand. "Pigs."

43

"It could have been anyone."

"I expect he did it to her here too."

"You're a little bit obsessed. Leave them alone. If they enjoy it."

"It spoils everything," said Monika. She balled up the wrapper and threw it in the bushes. "How do you do it? You're not a monk. How long have you been on your own?"

"Half a year . . . eight months. How do I do what?"

"It's so strange. It's nice, it doesn't cost anything, and you can do it anywhere. And yet . . ."

"I don't know . . . Really—everywhere . . ."

"In principle," said Monika. "Where was the craziest place that you slept with a woman?"

We had hung our towels up to dry on a tree, and were lying on the grassy bank. Monika turned toward me, looked at me, and smiled.

"It was just I didn't have any respect for you then," she said. "I liked you all right. But if I don't have any respect for a man . . ."

"What about now?" I asked.

Some clouds had drawn up, and when they passed in front of the sun, the temperature cooled quickly. We packed our things together, and moved off. The wind was gusting, but the water was almost still and very dark, and made little sucking sounds against the thin aluminum sides of our canoe. In some places it curled up, as over some shallows. Then we saw a flash of lightning, and we counted the seconds till the thunder, and we knew there was a storm at hand. I remembered my childhood, when the lifeguard had got us all out of the water when there was a storm coming. Then on the shore, just ahead of us, we spotted one of the little shelters they set up for canoeists here and there along the river. When we moored our boat, the waves were already high, and then all at once it started to rain. We pulled the boat onto the shore, covered it over with a tarpaulin, and ran for shelter.

"Where do you reckon the others are now?" I asked.

"No idea," said Monika. "Struck by lightning, for all I care."

The rain fell. We sat in the shelter for hours. Monika leaned against me, and I put my arm around her. Some time, we both fell asleep. Later on, we got the camping stove out of the boat, and made coffee and smoked the last of my cigarettes.

"What will we do if it doesn't stop raining?" I asked.

"Oh, it always stops eventually," said Monika.

It had gotten cold, and we could barely see the opposite bank through the teeming rain. It was like sitting in a room with walls of water. Gradually, it lessened, and we caught a glimpse of a low-angled sun. We paddled on. The river narrowed, and the current increased. We passed under a solitary bridge that water was still dripping off. In some places, trees had toppled into the river, and we had to squeeze by them. That night, we had trouble finding a campsite. By the time we finally did, mist was already rising off the water. We tried, unsuccessfully, to light a fire.

The next morning the sun was shining, but round about noon it began to rain again. A fisherman we met as we carried the boat around a little lock warned us that the weather would stay like this now. And it really did rain all that day, into the evening, when we put up our tent. Everything was wet, and this time we didn't try and cook, we just ate crispbread and ham with sweet mustard.

I couldn't sleep for a long time that night, but it didn't bother me. I listened to the rain falling on the taut canvas and thought of the time I was in love with Monika, and all that had passed since then. It rained all that night, and it was raining the next morning, and through most of that day as well. When it finally stopped, we had long since stopped bothering about it.

The river levels were high now, and the water was murky with particles of earth. The river was narrow at this point, and the current was so strong that the water seemed to roar, and we stopped using our paddles except to keep from running into anything. When we came around a corner, we saw a canoe on the bank, with bags, mats, and a couple of sleeping bags next to it. There was a big dent on it.

"I think they must have capsized," said Monika. "Our two fuckers. Shall we go see?"

"Do you want to?" I asked.

"They might need help," she said. "It's our duty as citizens."

We allowed ourselves to drift past the spot, turned, and made our way back to the bank against the current. "Hallo!" called Monika. "Michael, Sandra, are you there?" We heard nothing. Monika said she was going to have a little look around, and would I make some coffee. Then she found Michael, and called me.

"Sandra's gone to get help," said Michael, "she headed into the forest."

We helped him to get up. The three of us couldn't squeeze through the trees, but it turned out Michael wasn't in such a bad way as we'd initially supposed. He was able to walk unaided, but he had a limp, and favored his bare foot. By the time we were beside the river, the water for coffee was boiling. We only had two cups. Monika and I shared one, and gave the other one to Michael. After a few swallows, he began to talk.

"There was a fallen tree lying across the river. Up ahead. We took the corner too fast, and were unable to avoid it."

They had rammed the tree, and the canoe had turned sideways, tipped up, and immediately filled with water. They had jumped out of the boat, Michael said, the water wasn't deep at that place, but all their things had fallen into the river. Their food was gone, and the camping stove and the paddles as well. All they'd been able to save had been a few things that had bobbed on the surface for a while.

Monika asked if he wanted something to eat. He said he wasn't hungry. When we broke out our things, he ate with us after all. Then we decided to paddle on to find a place where there was more room for our tent. But Michael refused to get into a boat again.

"But how are you going to get away from this place, if not by boat?" asked Monika. I looked up the map. The nearest road was about three miles away. From there, it was at least another six to the nearest settlement.

"When did Sandra go?" I asked.

"Yesterday," said Michael. "No, it was this morning, in the early hours."

"We would get lost in the forest," said Monika, "at least on the river there's only one way to go."

Things got a little tight in the tent. Michael lay upside down next to Monika and me. I lent him a pair of socks. His sleeping bag was damp, and it smelled moldy in the tent. Michael fell asleep immediately, and started breathing heavily and rhythmically.

"I think he must have a fungus or something. Normal people's feet don't smell so bad," Monika whispered into my ear.

"It's his sleeping bag, I think," I whispered.

Then Monika started laughing quietly, and saying: "Oh, give it to me, oh, oh."

"Ssh, he'll hear."

She unzipped my sleeping bag, and groped for me.

"Just to warm my hands," she said.

"They're ice cold."

"That's the disadvantage of being alone."

I slept badly that night. When I woke up the next morning, Michael wasn't in the tent. I could hear him walking about outside. My sleeping bag was damp, and I felt cold.

"Are you awake?" Monika asked beside me.

"Yes," I said. "What's he doing?"

"What are you doing?" Monika called out.

"I'm looking for my shoe," Michael called back.

We crawled out of the tent. The weather was slightly better. It was still cloudy, but at least it had stopped raining. There was a thin mist between the trees and over the river. The air smelled of moldering wood. I put on some water to heat.

"This is the end of our coffee," I said. "We've just got powdered milk left."

"And mushrooms and roots," said Monika. "This is where the universal law kicks in."

Michael didn't say anything.

"We should start off before it begins raining again," said Monika.

"I'm not getting in a boat again," said Michael.

"Don't be childish," said Monika.

He stood up and disappeared into the forest. When we called after him to come back, he called out that he had to find his shoe first. He knew exactly where he had lost it. We packed our things, and also those of Sandra and Michael. We roped their canoe to ours. When we were done, we called Michael again. He made no reply, but we heard him in the underbrush nearby.

"If we don't set out now, we won't get there today," said Monika. "Come on, let's get him."

We followed Michael into the forest. As we got closer to him, he moved away, and when we went faster, he went faster as well.

"That's enough now," called Monika. "Stop right where you are."

"We have to wait for Sandra," he called back. At least he had stopped walking. When we had caught him up, he said it again: "We have to wait for Sandra."

"Why didn't the two of you just wait for us," I said. "You knew we weren't far behind."

"Sandra said you wouldn't stop," said Michael, "just because we overtook you. She thought you'd be mad at us. And because she hadn't tied the baggage on. She said you'd laugh at us."

"Are you crazy?" said Monika. "This isn't some kind of competition. Cow."

Michael bent down.

"My shoe must be very nearby," he said with a pathetic voice.

"Fuck your shoe," said Monika. I'd never seen her so angry. I could hear that it had begun raining again, but the drops couldn't get through the thick canopy of leaves. "We're going on now. And you're coming with us. We can leave a note for her."

"What about my shoe?"

"Leave it," screamed Monika. "We couldn't sleep all night because of your stinking feet. You must have got a fungal infection or something. And now we're going."

Michael was cowed and silent, and followed along behind us. Monika scribbled a note on a piece of paper, put it in a polythene bag, and attached that to a tree at eye level. She seemed to have calmed down.

"This isn't a game," she said to Michael. "This is a big, wild forest. You can die here, you know, just like an animal."

Our canoe was now low in the water. For a while the river snaked through the forest in tight curves, and then it widened out again, and it was easier to make headway. Toward noon, the sun briefly broke through the clouds. The trees were still dripping with moisture, and in the boat it smelled of our wet things. Once, we saw a hat caught in the boughs of a fallen tree in the water, and Michael said: "That's my hat."

Monika and I didn't say anything, and, though it would have been easy to fish it out, we carried on. The current grew weaker. We were now passing through tall rushes, and finally we got out onto a big lake. In the haze we couldn't make out the opposite shore. Monika looked at the map.

"The campsite is on the eastern shore, about six miles from here," she said. "If we keep going, we should get there tonight."

The wind was against us, and the canoe we were towing slowed us down as well. Monika and I paddled. Michael sat silently in the middle of the boat. Once I told him he should spell Monika. But he was so clumsy with the paddle that she soon took it out of his hands again. The wind grew fresher, and the waves lapped almost over the edge of the boat. We made barely any progress.

"At least when it was raining, there wasn't any wind," I said.

"Come on, don't give up," said Monika.

After that, we didn't speak any more. The shore was all overgrown with reeds, and it all looked the same. Once, we steered the boat into the reeds, and stopped to eat some ham and crispbread. Then we paddled on. It was past seven before we finally reached the campsite. There was a man on the shore, who helped us get the boats onto land.

Michael vanished as soon as we had landed. Monika and I scrubbed our canoe clean. When we carried it overhead to the boathouse, we saw Michael and Sandra walking across the campsite in a tight embrace. They didn't look in our direction. We put up our tent close to the shore, in the middle of people's caravans.

I was showering when I saw Michael once more. He was wearing some plastic sandals, and shaving. He gave me a barely audible greeting.

"I expected Sandra to come at the head of a rescue party," I said.

"She was going to come back for me," he said.

When I got back to the tent, Monika was gone. The socks I had lent Michael were airing on the line. I threw them in the nearest garbage can. Monika came, bringing a bottle of Portuguese wine, which she dug up somewhere.

"I ran into Sandra while I was showering," she said. "She was missing a tooth, at the front, in the middle. She didn't say a word to me."

We boiled some rice, opened a can of tuna, and drank the wine. Then, when it was almost completely dark, we walked down to the lake. We sat down on the pier.

"Do you think she would just have left him out there?" Monika asked.

"I don't know," I said. "Maybe because of the shoe."

"And what about the tooth?"

Music drifted softly from the garden restaurant, and there was the sound of TV from one of the caravans. Otherwise, it was quiet.

"Strange," I said, "do you remember there being any mosquitoes?"

Monika drew up her legs, and rested her face on her knees. She looked over the lake water for a long time. Then she turned her head, looked at me, and said: "Things always happen when you least expect them to."

"I didn't think anything like this would happen to us," I said.

"Who knows," said Monika, and she smiled. "Actually, I quite fancy sleeping with you. But only if you promise not to fall in love with me again."

PASSION

Whenever I think of Maria, I think of the evening she cooked for us. The rest of us were already sitting down at the table in the garden, and Maria stood in the doorway, with a flat dish in her hands. Her face was flushed from the heat in the kitchen, and she was beaming with pride in her work. Just at that moment, I felt incredibly sorry for her, and for the whole world, and for myself too, and I loved her more than I had ever loved her before. But I didn't say anything, and she set the food down on the table, and we ate it.

We had gone to Italy as a group, Stefan and Anita, Maria and me. It had been Maria's idea to visit the village of her grandfather. Her grandfather had emigrated to Switzerland many years ago as a young man, and even Maria's father had only known their former home as a vacation place.

We stayed in a small, slightly run down rental cottage, in the middle of a pine-wood near the sea. There were other cottages dotted about the wood, most of them bigger and handsomer than ours. Not far away was a coastal promenade, with restaurants, hotels, and shops. The old part of the village was back from the coast, at the foot of some hills. We spent most of our time in the new part, in our cottage, because we didn't have a car. Only once, after a late breakfast, did we call a taxi and visit the old village.

There was no one on the streets. From time to time a car drove by. We heard kitchen noises through an open window, and once we saw two black-clad women. Maria wanted to ask them about her grandfather, but before we could get near them they had vanished into one of the houses. We found a little bar that was open. We sat down at a table, and had something to drink. Maria asked the bar owner whether a family bearing her name lived in the village. He shrugged his shoulders and said he was from the north, and only knew the customers at the bar. And even with them, he mostly just knew their nicknames and Christian names.

Then we went to the graveyard, but there was no memento there of Maria's family either. We didn't find her name on any of the tombstones or any of the burial urns.

"Are you sure we're in the right village?" asked Stefan. "I always thought most Italians came from Sicily."

Maria didn't reply.

"Everything's so sleepy," said Stefan. "Your relatives could at least have gotten up if you've come all this way to visit them."

"Are you disappointed?" I asked.

"No," said Maria. "It's a beautiful village."

"Did you feel anything?" asked Anita. "I don't know, roots. Maybe there are some . . . I don't know, cousins of cousins still living here?"

At first we thought we would stay there a bit longer, but there was nothing for us to do, and we didn't see any restaurant where we could have gotten something to eat. We walked back, trekked along endless paths across a hot plain without any shelter from the sun. Once, a man rode past us on a motor scooter. He waved and shouted something I didn't understand. We waved back, and he disappeared in a white cloud of dust.

"Maybe he was a relative of yours," said Stefan, and grinned.

Ever since we'd arrived in Italy, it had been hot, so hot that not even the shadows of the trees offered any cool. In the daytime we were sleepy, but at night we hardly slept because of the heat and the cicadas, whose cries were so loud it was as though there'd been some calamity. I think we all wished we could have been back home, in the cool forests or the mountains, even Maria. But there was no way out of the heat, we were trapped in it, in our indolence, and unless the weather broke, our only hope was that the holidays would pass as soon as possible.

We hadn't done anything for days. Then Anita heard there was a riding stable somewhere nearby. She had enjoyed riding as a child, and she wanted to try it again. Stefan didn't feel like it, and Maria said she was frightened of horses.

Finally I told Anita I would go along with her. That evening she told all kinds of riding stories, and I had to sit backwards on a chair so she could show me how to use the reins, and what to do if the thing ran off with me.

When she saw the horses the next day, she was disappointed. They were old dirty beasts, standing around apathetically with drooping heads in front of their stables. We paid for the ride, and joined a little group of people waiting. After a while, a girl in riding boots and tight pants came out. She said something in Italian, handed each of us a whip, and allocated us our horses. She showed off in front of us, and talked to the horses as if it was they that had paid for us. A young man strolled across the yard toward us. Even before reaching us he called out a greeting, and asked whether we all spoke Italian. When a few said they didn't, he said in English: "We will explore the beautiful landscape on horseback."

He helped us into our saddles, jumped up himself, and rode off. He had briefly explained to us how to steer the horses, but regardless of what we did they trotted slowly along in Indian file. I felt ridiculous.

We rode through a dense forest. Everywhere in among the trees, there was rubbish in the underbrush, plastic bottles, an old bicycle, a defunct washing machine. The tracks we followed were deeply marked into the ground, because they had been taken so many times. I rode at the back of the column, and sometimes my horse stopped to nibble at bushes by the path. Then our leader would turn around and shout: "Hit him!" And if I didn't hit the horse hard enough, he would hit his own and shout: "Hit him harder!"

Anita, who was riding in front of me, turned and laughed. She said: "You're not hurting him."

I could feel the warmth of the great animal in my legs, which I pressed against his flanks, and the movements of his muscles. Sometimes I held the flat of my hand against his neck.

Our ride lasted barely half an hour. Anita and I had brought our swimming things. We got changed under the trees.

"I can't wear my clothes anymore," I said, "they stink so."

"I like the smell," said Anita. "I wish I could start riding all over again. It's only the riders I don't like. They're only interested in horses. And sex."

I said, "I think it's the smell that does it," and Anita laughed. We climbed up the steep dunes. Our feet sank into the soft sand. Anita went ahead of me, and I thought I would like to clasp her neck in my hand, and feel her warmth. Then she slipped over. I caught her by the waist, coming from behind her, stumbled over myself, and we both fell down. We laughed and helped each other up. We had been sweating, and sand stuck to our bodies. Before we went on, we helped to get it off each other's backs and arms.

We didn't stay long at the beach. It was dirty here, and the water was murky and too warm and smelled bad. It was much too hot now, and there were too many people there. When we got back to the house, we found Stefan and Maria had gone out. The blinds had been rolled down. It was dark, but no cooler than it was outside.

Still in our swimming things, we slumped down on Maria's and my bed. I looked at Anita. She raised her arms over her head, stretched, and yawned with closed mouth. "It's my favorite time," she said, "when you can lie down in the dark in the daytime, and not have to do anything."

"On days like this, I wish I could be an animal," I said. "I only want to drink and sleep. And wait for it to cool down some time."

Anita turned to face me. She propped herself up on one elbow, and cradled her head in her hand. She said she and Stefan had grown apart. Their relationship was boring. Stefan was boring. He couldn't get enthusiastic over anything with her. It was typical that he hadn't wanted to go riding with her. Even though she hadn't minded finally. "It's much more fun with you."

"I always thought you were the perfect couple."

"Who knows," said Anita, "maybe we were. And now we aren't anymore. What about you two?"

"So-so," I said. "I sometimes catch myself looking at other women. It's not a good sign, it seems to me. Maria must notice, but she doesn't say anything. She takes it. And I feel guilty."

"I noticed," said Anita, and she laughed, and let herself fall onto her back.

And then it got even hotter. In the morning the air was clear, but by noon everything had disappeared into a milky-white haze, as if the country below us were slowly going up in a smoldering fire. For the next few days we did absolutely nothing. Sometimes we got down to the sea early in the morning, or in the evening as the sun was going down. We did our shopping before the stores closed down for the afternoon, bought cheese and tomatoes, unsalted bread, and cheap wine in big liter bottles. Then we sat around and tried to read in the shade of the big pines in front of the house, but mostly we just dozed, or had futile conversations. In the evenings we cooked a meal, and over dinner we would quarrel noisily over matters that we didn't really know or care about. Maria was generally quiet during our debates. She listened as we quarreled, and when we made things up, she would get up and disappear somewhere with a book.

"I love the smell of summer," she said one time, "I don't even know what it is. It's more a feeling than a smell. You smell it with your skin, with your whole body."

"I used to have a better sense of smell," said Stefan. "Strange, isn't it? I even used to be able to smell the air, and the rain and the heat. Now I can hardly smell anything. It must be the pollution. I can't smell anything."

"You smoke too much," said Anita.

"Sometimes," Stefan said, "sometimes when I spit in the mornings, there's blood in my saliva. But I don't think it means anything. It might just be the wine."

"Dogs need more than half their brain capacity, just for smelling," I said.

"Everything's so complicated," said Anita. "Things used to be simpler."

Maria said she was going down to the beach. The rest of us went on with the conversation for a while, and then we set off after her. It took us a long time to find her, sitting in the dark, looking out to sea. The crashing of the waves seemed to be louder now than in the daytime. Maria said: "When you get along with each other, you're even worse than when you're quarreling."

Sometimes, Maria would cook Italian recipes for us. Then she would do the shopping herself and spend hours in the kitchen, and not let anyone in. She would have liked to be a good cook, but she wasn't.

Maria suffered least from the heat, and I noticed her getting more impatient with the rest of us by the day. One evening she said she had rented a car for the next day, she wanted to go on a trip. We could come along if we wanted. Anita and Stefan were delighted, but I didn't feel like driving anywhere, and I said so. Maria didn't say much, beyond that she couldn't force me to come. I had drunk too much wine as I did every evening, and I said I was going to sleep. As I lay in bed, I could hear the others discussing their outing, what they wanted to see, where they thought they might go.

"We should set out early," Maria said, "so that we arrive before it gets really hot."

"I'll take the camera," said Stefan, and Anita said she wanted to buy herself a hat, a straw hat.

I thought I'd like to stay like that forever with the open window, listening to the others making plans. Then they blew out the candles and brought in the dirty dishes, quietly, so as not to disturb me. When Maria crept under the covers next to me, I pretended to be asleep already.

That was the evening I felt such sympathy for Maria, when I felt so sorry for her and for myself, and for the whole world. As I lay in bed now, unable to sleep, hearing Maria's breathing next to me, I again had the feeling of absolute meaninglessness, which was at once sad and liberating. I thought I would never feel anything other than this sympathy, this feeling of connection with everything.

The others were already gone by the time I woke up. The whole house smelled fresh of soap and deodorant. I put on some coffee. I had finished my cigarettes the night before, and I had resolved to give up smoking now. Then I saw Stefan's cigarettes lying out on the table, and I helped myself. I drank my coffee, and I walked through the woods into town to buy more cigarettes. It wasn't even nine o'clock, but it was already heating up, and there were people everywhere making their way to the beach.

When I got back the house seemed deserted, as though no one had lived in it for ages. From the garden next door, I heard children playing, and in the distance there were cars and motorbikes going by. The garden chairs were standing under the pines, where we'd left them yesterday in our quest for shade. They had our magazines on them, and open books, lying face down. In the top of a tree, a bird screamed very loudly and very briefly. The children were quiet now, or they had gone inside, or around to the front. I felt empty but I didn't feel like eating, and just smoked another cigarette.

In the time we'd been here, I'd gotten much less reading done than I'd thought I would. Now that I finally had time I yearned for life, but I was still happy not to be sitting in a stuffy car, or traipsing through a sleepy town, through pedestrian precincts full of sweaty tourists, or drinking coffee on a crowded café terrace. I felt lonely, the way you only feel lonely in summer, or when you're a kid. I felt all alone in a world that was full of groups and families and couples, who were all together somewhere, far away. I read, but before long I put my book down. I leafed through some of the magazines, then I made some more coffee, and smoked. It was noon by now, and I went inside to shave for the first time in many days.

I had started to worry about the others when they finally came back in the evening. They seemed to be feeling guilty for having had such a lovely day. They had already returned the car.

They walked through the garden into the house, laden with plastic bags and packages. Anita was wearing a straw hat, and Stefan had a kite. Maria gave me a kiss on the mouth. She was hot from the long drive, and she smelled of sweat.

We went down to the sea, where there was hardly anyone left now. The sun was just over the horizon. The others ran out into the shallow water. I sat on the sand and smoked, and watched them splashing each other. Anita still had her new hat on.

After a while, they came out of the water. Maria stopped just in front of me, and dried herself. Against the light, I could only see her outline. Then she tossed the damp towel at me and said: "Well, and did you have a nice day, you stick-in-the-mud?"

Only now did they begin to talk about their trip. Briefly, I regretted not having gone with them, not because it had been anything special but because it would have been nice to share the memory with them. I said I had spent the day reading, and maybe they felt a little envious of me. Anita said they had brought me something, a present. Stefan ran along the beach with his kite but there was no wind, and in the end he gave up. We stayed by the sea till the sun had gone down, and then we went into the house to eat.

All through supper, Maria kept making little digs at my sluggishness till I lost my temper and told her to stop it. Surely she could get through one day without me. But she said I was always boring like that, even at home. I got up and went out into the garden. I heard the others finish their meal in silence. Then Maria came out. She stood in the doorway and looked out at the trees. After a while she said: "Don't be so childish."

I said I wasn't hungry anymore, and she said she wanted to go for a walk with me, down on the beach.

It wasn't quite dark. We walked along the beach close to the water, where the sand was firm and it was easier to walk. For a long time we didn't speak. Then Maria said: "I've been looking forward all day to seeing you again."

"You should have said something yesterday," I said. "I had too much to drink, and I didn't feel like going anywhere. I don't like the heat."

"We're too different," said Maria. "I don't know. Maybe . . ."

"Surely we can manage to be apart for one day."

"It's not that," she said, and then, more in surprise than anger, she asked: "What do you want anyway . . . ?"

She stopped but I walked on, faster than before. She came after me.

"You always dramatize everything," I said. "I don't want anything."

"I'm not dramatizing anything," said Maria. "We just don't get along."

"What do you mean by that?"

"It's not your fault."

Maria stopped again, and this time I didn't walk on. I turned to face her. There was a jellyfish on the sand in front of her, a small, transparent mound of aspic. She nudged it with her foot.

"Silly things," she said. "They're beautiful when they're in the water. But when they get washed up onto the shore . . . there's nothing you can do for them."

She picked up a handful of sand and crumbled it onto the jellyfish. She waited.

Finally I said: "Do you want to . . . ?"

"When the sun shines, there won't be anything left of it," said Maria. She hesitated, and then she said yes.

"It's Italy," I said. "It's only because we're in Italy. Back home, everything will feel completely different."

"Yes," said Maria, "that's why."

She said she didn't feel good here. "It's not the heat. But I don't have any feeling of having come from here. It doesn't say anything to me. I can't imagine my grandfather living here. I can't even imagine my father coming here for vacation. I thought there'd be something here for me. But it's all completely foreign. And you . . . I have to feel I belong somewhere, with someone."

She turned and walked back. I sat down on the sand next to the dead jellyfish, and lit a cigarette. I stayed there smoking for a long time.

When I got back to the house, the others were still sitting outside, talking and drinking wine. I went inside without a word. Maria followed me. We stood together in front of the sofa in the living room, where Maria had made up a bed for herself. She didn't say anything, and I didn't either. I went into the bedroom, got undressed and lay down. I couldn't sleep for a long time.

I awoke because there was someone in the room. Outside, it was getting light. Maria was packing her things. She didn't make any effort not to make any noise. I watched her secretly, but when she turned toward me, I closed my eyes and pretended to be asleep. She carried her bag down into the living room and then came back once more and stood by the bed. She stayed there for a long time and then she left, closing the door softly behind her. I heard her making a phone call. After a while, a car drew up outside. It stopped, but the motor was running. Then I heard doors slam, and the car moved away. I stood up and went into the living room.

The sofa was empty. The bedclothes were folded up beside it on the floor. There was a piece of paper on the table. While I read it, Anita came out of her bedroom. She asked what was happening, and I said Maria had gone home.

"Something went wrong," I said. "I don't know what, I must have done something wrong."

"What time is it?" Anita asked.

"Six," I said.

"Is that all? I'm going back to bed for a while then."

We went back to our rooms. There was a T-shirt of Maria's next to the bed. I picked it up. It smelled of her, her sweat, her sleep, and for a moment I felt she was still there, that she'd just gone out for a while.

At breakfast we didn't talk about Maria not being there. But later, when Stefan went to the beach to try to get his kite to fly again, Anita asked me why Maria had left me: "Was it something to do with Italy?"

"Yes," I said, without much conviction, "it's all so complicated."

"Do you think you'll get back together?" Anita asked.

I said I didn't know, I wasn't even sure I wanted that.

Anita said she envied us really. "I've wanted to do that for such a long time. If I wasn't so passive . . ."

"I can't imagine her life without me," I said.

"That's always the way of it, but life always goes on somehow," said Anita.

Stefan came back. There hadn't been any wind, and as he was dragging the kite across the beach, a dog had grabbed at it and chewed it up. Anita grinned.

"You should have buried it on the spot," she said.

"When I was a kid I always longed for a kite," said Stefan, "but all I ever got were clothes and books and schoolbags."

"You haven't given me my present yet," I said, "the thing you brought back for me."

"Maria's got it," said Anita. "She must have taken it away with her."

"What was it?"

"I don't know. We weren't with her when she bought it." Maria had been all secretive, and hadn't wanted to tell anyone.

"I expect it was something stupid," said Stefan.

"Maybe she'll send it to me," I said, "or I'll call her."

It was the last day of our vacation. We packed our things and cleaned the house. There was sand all over. In the evening we went to the promenade. We wanted to go and eat in a restaurant.

"Why do Italians always keep their shutters down?" Stefan asked, as we passed through the settlement of vacation homes.

"With that heat . . ." said Anita.

"They do it at home too," said Stefan. "I used to have Italian neighbors. They always kept their shutters closed. And an enormous satellite dish on their balcony."

"Maybe homesickness," said Anita.

We strolled along the promenade. The sun had gone down, but it was still hot. There were tables and chairs out in front of the restaurants. There were big luminous signs showing the food they offered. The red was bleached, and the food all looked blue and unappetizing. One restaurant had fish and shellfish lying out in front of it, in baskets full of crushed ice.

"Can you smell anything?" Stefan asked. "I can't smell anything. Surely you should be able to smell it."

"If fish smells fishy, you shouldn't eat it," said Anita.

We were unable to decide on a restaurant, and we walked on to the end of the promenade. There we sat down on a low wall. The sky was empty, it looked locked up against the neon from all the restaurants. Stefan had lain down on the wall, and was resting his head on Anita's lap. She was stroking his hair. I sat next to her. Our shoulders were touching.

"Look at that star," said Stefan, "it must be a fixed star, it's so bright."

"It's an airplane," said Anita, "only airplanes give out that much light."

"Airplanes blink," said Stefan, "and they have red and green lights."

The bright light slowly moved across the sky. We were quiet, and watched it disappear into the west.

"It's a nice feeling," said Anita, "to think there are people up there, flying into the morning. Somewhere another day's beginning. Here it's still night, and they'll be seeing the sun already. The American sun."

"I feel I've been here for ever," said Stefan.

"I could live here," said Anita, "and do nothing but look at airplanes, and eat and read. I feel really at home here."

"I wonder where Maria is now," I said. "I wonder what she wanted to give me."

THE MOST BEAUTIFUL GIRL

After five mild, sunny days on the island, clouds started to mass. It rained overnight, and the next morning it was twenty degrees colder. I walked over the reef, a giant sandbar in the southwest, which was no longer land and not yet sea. I couldn't see where the water began, but I thought I had a sense of the curvature of the earth. Sometimes I crossed the tracks of another walker, though there was no one to be seen far and wide. Only occasionally a heap of seaweed, or a black wooden post corroded by seawater, sticking out of the ground. Somewhere I came upon some writing that someone had stamped in the wet sand with his bare feet. I followed the script, and read the word "ALIEN." In the distance I could hear the ferry, which was due to dock in half an hour. It was as though I could hear its monotonous vibration with my whole body. And then it began to rain, a light and invisible shower that wrapped itself around me like a cloud. I turned and walked back.

I was the only guest staying at the pension. Wyb Jan was sitting in the lobby with Anneke, his girlfriend, drinking tea. The room was full of model ships, Wyb Jan's father had been a sea captain. Anneke asked me if I wanted a cup of tea. I told them about the writing on the sand.

"Alien," I said. "It's exactly how I felt on that sandspit. As strange as if the earth had thrown me off." Wyb Jan laughed, and Anneke said: "Alien is a girl's name in Dutch. Alien Post is the most beautiful girl on the island."

"You're the most beautiful girl on the island," Wyb Jan said to Anneke, and kissed her. Then he tapped me on the shoulder and said: "When the weather's like this, it's best to stay indoors. If you go out, it might drive you crazy."

He went into the kitchen to get me a cup. When he came back, he switched on a lamp and said: "I'll put an electric heater in your room."

Anneke said: "I wonder who wrote that. Do you think Alien's found herself a boyfriend at long last?"

WHAT WE CAN DO

Evelyn had suggested a café with a silly name like Aquarium or Zebra or Penguin, I can't remember. She often ate there in the evenings, she said. When I arrived, only two of the tables were occupied. I sat down near the door and waited. I looked at the menu. It was one of those places where the dishes have strange names, and the portions are on the small side.

We could go out for a beer together, I had said to Evelyn when we shook hands on my last day at work. It was what I said to everyone on that day, without ever really meaning it. Evelyn said she didn't drink beer, and I said it didn't have to be beer. And then she said sure, and when was convenient for me. I didn't have any option but to make a date with her.

When Evelyn finally turned up, a quarter of an hour late, I was pretty drunk.

"Would you mind if we sat over there?" she said. "I always sit over there."

She greeted the guests at the other tables by name.

"Do you live here or something?" I asked.

Evelyn found it hard to choose a dish. Even when the waitress had already taken her order, she changed her mind again.

"Don't you know the menu by heart, then?" I asked.

Evelyn laughed. "I always have the same thing," she said. After that, she didn't say anything, and just beamed at me. I talked about God knows what. By the time the food finally arrived, I had no idea what else I could have spoken about. Evelyn seemed not to have any interests. When I asked her about any hobbies she might have, she said: "I always wanted to be good at singing."

"Do you take singing lessons?"

She said: "No, that's too expensive for me."

"Are you in a choir?"

"No, I feel ashamed to sing in front of other people."

"Well, that's not exactly an ideal basis for a career as a singer," I joked, and she laughed.

"No, I just wish it was something I was good at."

No sooner had we drunk our coffee than Evelyn said the restaurant was closing in a quarter of an hour.

"Shall we go and have a nightcap somewhere?" I asked, out of politeness, when we were standing on the pavement.

"I don't like to go to bars," said Evelyn. "I hate the smoke. But if you like, I'll make us both a hot chocolate."

She blushed. So as not to make the situation still more embarrassing, I said if she had coffee, I'd be happy to go along. She said she had instant, and I said that was fine.

"Doesn't your girlfriend mind you going out with other women?"

"I don't have a girlfriend."

"I don't either," said Evelyn, "I mean, a boyfriend. Just now."

Evelyn lived on the third floor of a tenement block. She looked in her mail box. It seemed just to be a kind of reflex, because she must have emptied it earlier in the evening. As she stepped into her apartment, she gestured clumsily and said: "Well, welcome to my palace."

She led me to the living room, pointed to the sofa, and told me to make myself at home. I sat down, but as soon as she'd disappeared into the kitchen, I got up again and looked around. The room was furnished with light clunky pine furniture. On the bookshelf were about thirty illustrated volumes on all kinds of topics, a few travel books, and lots of novels with bright covers, and titles with women's names in them. There were costume dolls lying and standing around all over. On the walls were felt-tip drawings of cats and flower pots, which I assumed Evelyn had made herself.

It took a long time for Evelyn to have the coffee and hot chocolate ready. The coffee was much too weak. I told some story about something or other, and then Evelyn suddenly started talking about an illness she suffered from. I can't remember what it was, but it was something to do with her digestion. Only then did it occur to me that she smelled bad. Perhaps that was why she reminded me of a plant, some potted plant that was missing something, either light or fertilizer, or else was too heavily watered.

After that, Evelyn was very quiet, but when I got up to go she suddenly started talking.

She said: "I get these letters, from a man. He seems to know me, I don't know."

A man who called himself Bruno Schmid had been writing to her for months, she said, and I wasn't sure whether she wasn't just putting on airs. But she did seem genuinely disturbed.

"I keep them hidden," she said, and she pulled down a small box lined with marbled paper from the bookshelf. There was a bundle of letters inside it. She took out the top one and passed it to me. I read.

"Dear Miss Evelyn,

I like you, I find your proximity appealing. Are we in any danger of wanting something unbeknown to ourselves? It should be neither sinful nor lethal. Children need parents to ward off dangers. I have never been able to get away from their warnings. My faith takes up a fair part of my time, and of my fortune. But there is much left, which I would like to share. I sense you have unfulfilled hopes, and I would like to learn about them. I wonder what I can do for you.

Best wishes . . ."

"He always writes the same things," said Evelyn, looking at me beseechingly.

"Some poor madman," I said.

"What does he mean when he says it shouldn't be lethal?"

"Life always ends in death," I said, "but I don't think he's dangerous."

"Sometimes I wish I was old already. Then it would all be over. All that disquiet."

"Are you scared of him?"

"The world is full of maniacs."

To distract her, I asked her about her dolls. She said she collected dolls in national costume. She already had thirty of them, mostly given her by her parents, who traveled a lot.

"Have you gone on to a new job already?" she asked.

"I wanted to take a trip around the world."

"Perhaps you could bring me back a doll," she said. "I'd pay you, of course."

Then she disappeared to the bathroom, and didn't come back for a long time. When I left, I kissed Evelyn on both cheeks.

"Will we see each other again?" she asked.

"I'm not quite sure when I'm leaving," I said. "You can call me. If I'm still here, that is."

Two weeks later, I had a call from Evelyn. I had given up my plans for going around the world, and decided to go to the south of France for a few weeks instead. Evelyn asked if I'd like to come over for supper. She had asked a few people.

"People from work," she said. "It's my thirtieth birthday. Please come."

Even though I had no desire to see my former colleagues again, I said I would come. I had a feeling I owed Evelyn something.

When I turned up on the evening in question, I was the first person there. Evelyn was wearing a short skirt that didn't suit her, and an old-fashioned apron over it.

"I had to shine the doorknobs this morning," she said. "It was an idea of Max's. It's something they do in Germany. When a woman gets to be thirty and is still single, she has to polish doorknobs."

She said some of our colleagues had put mustard on the doorknobs over the whole floor.

"They want to keep on doing it now. It'll be Chantal's turn next. And men have to clean the stairs. You're only allowed to stop when someone kisses you."

She said it had been ghastly, but I had the feeling she had quite enjoyed being the center of attention for a while. She showed me a long chain of paper cartons she had had to wear round her neck.

"Because I'm now what the Germans call an old box," she said, and laughed.

"And who kissed you?" I asked.

"Max," she said. "After a couple of hours. He's one of the guests."

The other guests all came together, Max and his girl-friend Ida, Evelyn's boss Richard and his wife Margrit. They seemed pretty happy. Max said they had stopped in a bar in the neighborhood, and drunk an aperitif. They had gone in together to buy Evelyn a present. He handed Evelyn a box, and the four of them started to sing: "Happy birthday to you."

Evelyn blushed and smiled sheepishly. She wiped her hands on her apron and shook the package.

"I wonder what it can be?" she said.

Inside the box was a cookbook, *Recipes for Lovers* or *Cooking for Two* or something of the sort.

"There's something else in there as well," said Max. Evelyn pulled aside some crumpled crepe paper. Under it was a vibrator in the shape of a colossal orange penis. She stared into the box, without touching the thing.

"It was Max's idea," said Richard. He was embarrassed, but Margrit, a heavily made-up woman of fifty or so, laughed shrilly and said: "Every woman needs one. Especially once you're married."

"I got this one out of Ida's collection," said Max, and Ida: "Max, you're so awful. You know I don't have any-thing like that."

"Not anymore," said Max, "not anymore. We've sup-plied the batteries as well."

"I have to go to the kitchen," said Evelyn, "otherwise the supper will burn."

She put the crepe paper back in the box, shut the lid, and went out.

"I told you it was a bad idea," whispered Richard.

"Ah, nonsense," said Max, "it'll be good for her. You'll see, in a month she'll be a different person."

Margrit laughed shrilly again, and Ida said: "Max, you're disgusting."

"Anyway, Evelyn's got you now," Max said to me.

Then they started talking about work, and I went into the kitchen to help Evelyn.

She had gone to a lot of trouble, but the food was nothing special. Even so, the atmosphere was relaxed. Max told dirty jokes that made Richard and his wife laugh. Ida seemed to be drunk after her first glass of wine, and didn't say much except that Max was awful. Evelyn was busy serving the food, and taking out the dirty dishes. I was bored. After supper, we drank tea and instant coffee. Then Max said we should leave Evelyn on her own now, she was probably dying to try out her new present. The four of them got up and put their coats on. I said I would help Evelyn with the washing up. Max said something off-color, and Ida said he was disgusting. Evelyn showed them down to the front door, and I heard loud laughter from the stairwell, and then the door crashing shut.

When Evelyn came back she said: "I can wash up tomorrow." Then she said she wanted to freshen up. It seemed like a sentence from a film or a cheap novel. I didn't know what it meant, or what I was supposed to say. She disappeared into the bathroom, and I waited. I wanted to put on some music, but I couldn't find any CDs I wanted to listen to, so I left it. I took down an illustrated volume about the Kalahari Desert, and settled down on the sofa. I wished I could be somewhere else, preferably at home.

I heard Evelyn go from the bathroom to the bedroom, and then she finally came back to the living room. She was in her underwear, which was white and solid and shiny. She had slippers on her feet. She stopped in the doorway, leaned against the doorjamb, and pushed one leg in front of the other. I had just been looking at photographs of gophers, skinny, catlike creatures that stand over their burrows and look into the distance. I set the book down next to me on the sofa. We didn't speak. Evelyn went red and looked down at the floor. Then she said: "Would you like another coffee? I think there's some hot water left."

"Sure," I said.

She disappeared into the kitchen. I followed her. She took down the jar of instant coffee, and I held out my cup. She tipped in way too much coffee powder, and poured in hot water. Oily scum formed in the cup. I saw Evelyn had tears in her eyes, but neither of us said anything. I sat down at the kitchen table, and she sat down opposite me. She sat slumped on her chair, with eyes closed, shaking. I looked at her. Her bra was too big. The two arced cups stood out in front of her breasts like shields. Once again, I noticed her disagreeable smell.

"Are you gay?" she asked.

"No," I said, and wished I was drunk.

"I've got a headache."

"Are you not cold?"

"No," she said. She stood up and folded her arms across her chest, holding her upper arms in her hands. I followed her into the bedroom. She lay down on the bed, and started sobbing silently into the pillows. Her body jerked convulsively. I sat down on the side of the bed.

"What's the matter?" I asked.

"I don't know," she said.

I ran my hand down her back, and along her legs down to her feet.

"You've got a pretty back," I said.

Evelyn sobbed aloud, and I said: "A pretty back has its attractions."

She turned over and for a moment lay quite relaxed in front of me, her arms by her sides. She took slow, deep breaths, and looked up at the ceiling. Then she said: "It's no good. And it's not going to get any better."

"You mustn't expect too much," I said. "Happiness consists of wanting what you get."

"I want a glass of wine," she said, and sniffed and slowly sat up. There was a packet of Kleenex beside the bed, and she took one out and blew her nose. Then she got up and went over to the chair where her dress was hanging. She hesitated briefly, and then pulled out a pair of jeans and a blouse from the wardrobe. I watched her get dressed with practiced movements. When she bent over to smooth the stockings over her knees, I momentarily felt like sleeping with her.

"We're at our best when we do what we can," I said, "what we've always been able to do."

Evelyn turned to me and said, buttoning her jeans: "But I don't like what I do. And I like what I am even less. And it's just getting worse."

We went back into the living room, and she got a bottle of wine from the kitchen. Then she went over to the stereo, pulled a few CDs off the rack, and put them back. Then she switched on the radio. A Tracey Chapman song was playing. I went to the bathroom. From the corridor I heard Evelyn slowly singing along: "Last night I heard a screaming . . ."

She didn't sing well, and when I walked back into the living room, she stopped.

"I have to go home," I said. "Will you be all right?"

"Yes," she said, "I'll be fine. Will you do me a favor?"

She got the carton with the vibrator and gave it to me.

"Will you chuck this in a bin somewhere. I don't want it anywhere around tonight."

"What shall I do about the batteries?" I asked. She didn't answer.

"Okay," I said. "I can see myself out."

When I turned around at the top of the stairs, Evelyn was still standing in the doorway. I waved, and she smiled and waved back.

THE TRUE PURE LAND

When I moved in, the room's single window was so dirty that the room seemed twilit even in the middle of the day. Even before I unpacked my suitcase, I cleaned the window. When Chris came home in the evening, he laughed and called Eiko.

He said: "Look and see what our guest has done."

"The Swiss are very clean," said Eiko.

I laughed. That was in April. I had gone to New York because I was fed up with Switzerland. I was lucky enough to find a job for six months working in a travel agency that belonged to a Swiss woman. But it was so badly paid I could only afford a very cheap room. The building was on the corner of Tieman Street and Claremont Avenue, on the edge of Spanish Harlem. On the other side of the street were tall dilapidated brick buildings inhabited almost entirely by Hispanics.

The first week I went to some bar or other every night with people from work. On the weekends I was mostly on my own. Chris and Eiko would be visiting friends or somewhere in the city, and the apartment was peaceful and empty.

One rainy Sunday morning, I set off to explore the area. I headed south down Riverside Drive. The traffic was heavy but there were hardly any pedestrians, and I enjoyed the feeling of being on my own. Somewhere around 100th Street, I saw a bigger than life-size statue of a Buddhist monk in a niche in a house. He was standing barefoot behind a black fence, looking out at the Hudson River. The rain started coming down harder, and I turned back and went home.

In the store on the ground floor of our building I bought the Sunday edition of the New York Times, and spent the rest of the day reading it. When I sat down on the window seat in the evening to smoke a cigarette, I noticed a window with a red light in the house opposite. I saw the slender form of a woman, leaning down over a lamp to switch it off. Just afterwards, there was a flash at the back of the room. Then the room remained dark.

I wasn't thinking about the woman in the house opposite when I sat down in the window again for a smoke a few days later. The room was once again illuminated by the red standard lamp, and once again I saw her. She was moving slowly about the room, as if dancing. Her window was open but I couldn't hear music, only the sounds of traffic from Broadway and the occasional rumble of the subway on its viaduct. I smoked a second cigarette. The woman stopped dancing. As she shut the window, I had the brief impression that she was looking across at me. But she was about twenty yards away, and I could only make out her outline. She draped a cloth over the lamp, and then she left the part of the room that I could see into.

Down on the street, some kids were rocking parked cars till their alarms went off. The wail of the sirens mingled with the noise of the city, but no one seemed to pay it any mind. I tossed my butt down on the street, shut the window, and lay down.

Chris came from Alabama. He had been living in New York for several years. He had studied politics, and had a badly paid job with a church organization. Eiko was still studying. She described herself as a heathen to irritate Chris. She was a Marxist and a feminist.

"If my mother calls," Eiko told me once, "you're not to say anything about Chris. She doesn't know I have a boyfriend. I told her you're both gay."

Chris laughed, and I laughed as well. "And what if she comes by?" I asked.

"My parents live out on Long Island," said Eiko. "They never come to Manhattan."

Sometimes I went out for a beer with Chris. Then he would complain about Eiko's political views and her stubbornness, and the way she had a different view of their relationship from his. He loved her, but he wasn't sure she loved him back. "She doesn't believe in anything," he said, "not even me."

I had stopped going out with my colleagues. After work I usually went straight home. Then I would sit in the window and smoke, and sometimes I saw my dancer.

Summer came, and it got unbearably hot on the streets. Eiko went back to Japan for three months. Before she left, she and Chris invited me to supper.

"Will you look after Chris for me while I'm away," said Eiko. "He's so helpless on his own."

We drank Californian wine, and sat up past midnight talking.

"Chris is really warped," said Eiko. "He likes country music."

Chris was embarrassed. "My parents always used to listen to it. It's just nostalgia for me. I don't really like it."

"You've got to listen to it," said Eiko. "Home, sweet home."

She put in the cassette. Chris protested, but he made no move to take it out.

"No more from that cottage again will I roam, be it ever so humble, there's no place like home," sang a deep voice. I had never heard Eiko laugh so wholeheartedly. I laughed as well, and finally Chris did too, reluctantly and slightly shamefacedly.

My head was spinning from the wine and lots of cigarettes and all our talk as I finally turned in at about two in the morning. But I noticed right away that the light was still on in the window opposite. As I smoked a last cigarette, I saw the dancer lean over the lamp and switch it off. I kept watching a while longer, before finally switching off my own light, and going to sleep.

Eiko left, and Chris often came home late. Sometimes I could tell he'd been drinking. "I miss her," he said.

The first of August* was a Monday. My boss was organizing the celebrations for the Swiss Club, and gave us the afternoon off. A group of us went to the beach, which was almost deserted during the week. We swam, and as evening fell we lit a fire behind a sand dune and grilled some steaks. Someone had brought along a tape recorder, and was playing Swiss rock music.

I ate my steak and walked over the dune, and across the wide beach down to the sea. Sky, sand, and sea were almost indistinguishable now, all a dusty pink or tan color. I took my clothes off, and swam out till I could no longer see land beyond the waves. I felt I could swim on and on, till I got to Europe. Then for the first time since coming here, I wanted to go home. Suddenly I was afraid I might not make it back to land, and I turned and swam back. As I was climbing the dune again, I heard whispering voices. I saw one of my colleagues lying in the sand with his girlfriend. She had just recently come to America to visit him, and the pair of them had been lovey-dovey all evening.

It was after midnight when I got home. There were no lights on in the apartment, and it was very quiet. There

---

*National holiday in Switzerland.

was a whiff of marijuana in the air. Dirty dishes were piled up in the kitchen.

In the middle of August Chris went away on vacation. He was going to stay with his parents in Alabama.

"Look after yourself," I told him.

He laughed. "My mother will look after me. You'll see, I'll have put on ten pounds by the time I'm back."

It no longer cooled off at night. The city was swarming with tourists, but the subways were less crowded than usual. In my part of town, you could hear samba and salsa music till late at night. Everywhere people were sitting on their front steps talking. Young men stood around in groups, leaning on cars that weren't theirs. Young women strolled back and forth in twos and threes and looked around at the men and sometimes called out a few words to them. There were hardly any couples. I hadn't thought about my dancer for a long time, but now I looked at the women on the street and thought which one of them might be her.

A postcard came from Eiko. It was addressed to Chris, but I read it anyway. There was nothing in it of a personal nature. She signed off, "*Love, Eiko.*"

One evening toward the end of the month, I was sitting in my room in the twilight. Then I heard the wailing of sirens outside closer than I ever had yet. I looked out the window and saw firetrucks turning into our street. Men in protective clothing leaped out of the trucks, but then they just stood there without doing anything. They took off their black helmets, and wiped the sweat off their brows. They stood there individually posed, like statues.

A large crowd had assembled, and some of the firemen blocked off the end of the road. But that was all that happened. After a while, the sirens stopped their wail. I was going to shut the window, and then I saw my dancer standing on the fire escape of the house opposite. It was the first time I had ever seen her completely, though her face was indistinct in the dark. She was leaning on the railing, and looking across at me. As soon as she saw I had noticed her, she turned away. She was slender and not very tall. She had long black hair that fell over one shoulder, because of the way she was leaning on the fire escape. She was wearing a knee-length skirt and a tight top. She was barefoot. When she turned away after a while to climb back through the window into her room, the light from the red lamp caught her face momentarily. I was certain I had never seen her on the street.

After weeks of incessant heat, it finally started to cool down. The sky was still radiant blue, but at least there was usually a breeze blowing through the city streets now. When I rode out to the beach with friends on the weekends, the extensive parkland behind the dunes was almost deserted. Then we would just lay ourselves flat on the sand to be out of the wind, or else we would walk along the beach in our clothes and watch the gray water scoop up the sand.

One day, an empty Sunday, I finally decided to pay a visit to my dancer. I hadn't spoken to anyone for two days, and I felt completely wretched. It was a radiant afternoon as I crossed the street. I stopped in front of the building and lit a cigarette. It began to rain. First a couple of fat drops splashed down on the crooked cement slabs of the sidewalk, and then the heavens opened. I jumped into the little glazed-in porch where the doorbells were, and from where a further, locked door led to the stairwell.

Outside, the rain was teeming down, and spurting against the panes. There was a smell of drenched asphalt. I peered through the iron grille into the entrance hall, which was dark and silent. There was a mosaic tiled flooring, which had been patched with cement. The walls were ocher. In the background I saw the door of an elevator, and beside it a narrow staircase going up, dimly lit by the light through a grimy window. There was a stroller, and a rusty bike in a corner.

A woman with a dog emerged from the elevator, and came across the hallway toward me. She opened the door, held it open for me, and said: "This rain. You must have just missed it. Were you on your way to see someone in the building?"

I said: "I was just sheltering here till the rain stopped."

"I was going to walk the dog," she said, "but with this weather I'm not so sure . . . Where are you from?"

"Switzerland," I said.

"A beautiful country," she said, "so clean. I come from Puerto Rico. But I've been living here a long time. Years."

"Do you like it here?"

"I couldn't live in Puerto Rico, and I can't live here either," she said. "I don't know. I'm not going out in this. Good luck."

She went back to the elevator, dragging her dog after her. I slid my foot in the door, then took it back, and the door crashed shut. Once the rain eased, I ran back across the street. I was shivering. I took a hot shower, but it didn't do any good. I felt cold and damp in the apartment.

A week later, Chris came back. We spent a few nice evenings together, eating and talking till late. The day before Eiko was due back, we cleaned the place and listened to country music.

"Please don't tell her I've been smoking marijuana," Chris said.

"Of course I won't," I said, "it's none of my busines."

"We're friends," said Chris. "We men need to stick together."

"Stick together against who?" I asked, and thought: we're not friends.

Chris laughed. "I used to smoke a lot more. But since I met Eiko, I've almost given up. She doesn't approve. And I don't need it when I've got her."

Then Eiko came back, and Chris didn't have any time for me anymore. The two of them often invited their friends over, and I took myself to the movies, and when I was home I generally stayed in my room. On the weekends I would sometimes spend whole days reading, and only go out to buy beer or to pick up Chinese take-out. My interest in the dancer had faded. I tried not to think about her. Sometimes I still saw her. She was now often sitting at the back of her room, where I could only dimly make her out.

One evening, when I was sitting by the window smoking, someone called up to me from the street. I looked down and saw a young woman standing on the sidewalk with a poodle. She waved up at me.

"I've come on behalf of my friend," she called. "She lives opposite, and always sees you in the window."

"Yes," I called back, "I see her too."

"She would like to meet you," the woman called up, as if to stick up for her friend. "She didn't want me to tell you."

"Right," I called. I felt paralyzed. For a moment, neither of us spoke.

Then the woman said: "She's called Margarita. Do you want her number?"

She gave me the number and told me once more: "She didn't want me to tell you."

"Sure," I said, "it's nice that you came and told me anyway."

I looked across at the window with the red light, but I couldn't see the dancer. I sat down on my bed, and took a few deep breaths. Then I picked up the phone from the bedside table, and dialed the number.

"Hallo," I heard a warm woman's voice.

"Hallo," I said, "I'm the man in the window opposite."

The girl laughed in embarrassment.

"Your friend gave me your number."

"I didn't want her to," she said softly.

"Would you like to meet?" I asked.

"Yes," she said. "My name's Margarita."

"I know," I said, "what about right away?"

"Sure," she said. Her English wasn't very good.

"We could go for a beer."

She hesitated. Then she said: "Tomorrow."

"Okay, I'll be outside your house at eight o'clock," I said. "Is that good?"

"Yes. That's good."

"Goodnight, Margarita."

"Goodnight," she said.

I was nervous all the next day, and wondered whether I should turn up at all. At eight I was waiting outside Margarita's house, but she wasn't there. I waited for a quarter of an hour, then I went up to my room and called her number. I stood by the window, and kept my eyes on the street.

Margarita answered. "Hallo," she said.

"Hallo," I said. "I thought we were going to go out for a beer."

"Now?" she asked in surprise.

"It's eight o'clock."

"Eight o'clock."

"Yes."

"Are you at your window?" she asked. "Hang on, I'll wave."

I looked across at the dancer's room, but all I could see was the faint outline of the standard lamp. Then I heard Margarita's voice on the phone again.

"Did you see me?" she asked.

"No," I said.

"Top floor," she said, "middle apartment. Wait, I'll go out again."

"Oh, okay," I said in alarm.

I looked up at the top floor of the opposite building, but I still couldn't see anyone. Finally, two buildings along I spotted someone standing by the window, and waving both arms.

"Did you see me that time?" asked Margarita shortly after.

"Yes."

"I'm coming down now."

"Okay," I said. "I'll be right over."

Margarita was pretty and quite small. She was wearing jeans and a brightly colored blouse. I can't say I didn't like her, but she wasn't who I expected. She wasn't the woman I thought I'd known for months. We walked down the street together. As we turned into Broadway, I saw Chris coming the other way. There was nothing else to do but to introduce them to each other. Chris smiled and wished us a pleasant evening.

We went into the nearest bar, and sat down at a table. It was noisy. Margarita didn't understand much English. She said she came from Costa Rica, and had been in the States for a couple of months. She was living with her sister and brother-in-law. They both worked, and she was alone in the apartment all day. She was very bored. When I asked her if she was looking for a job, she became suspicious, and said she was here on vacation.

"What do you do with yourself all day?" I asked.

"I go to the beach," she said. "In Costa Rica there are very beautiful beaches."

"New York has some beautiful beaches as well," I said.

She laughed and shook her head in disbelief. "Palms," she said, "in Costa Rica. And the sand is so white."

I asked her how long she planned on staying, and she said she didn't know. I told her I came from Switzerland, but she didn't know where that was. The conversation was sticky, and we sat and looked at each other in silence, and drank our beers. Once, I picked up Margarita's hand, but then I let it drop again. She smiled at me, and I smiled back.

We said goodbye outside her building. I was going back to Switzerland soon, I explained, it was too bad. Margarita smiled. She seemed to understand.

"Thanks for the beer," she said.

"Good luck," I said.

For the next few days, I avoided the window. When I felt like a smoke, I went outside to Riverside Park. If it was raining, I sheltered at the tomb of General Grant.

Sometimes I went as far as 100th Street, and spent a long time in front of the statue of the Buddhist monk. The bronze plaque on the statue said it was a depiction of Shinran Shonin, the founder of the sect of the true pure land. It came from Hiroshima, where it had survived the first atom bomb. That evening, I asked Eiko about the sect of the true pure land.

"Do you want to be a Buddhist?" she asked.

"No," I said. "I don't want to be reincarnated."

Eiko said, according to Shinran's precepts it was enough to say the name Amida Buddha to be admitted to the pure land.

"Do you think there is a pure land?" I asked.

"Switzerland," said Eiko, and laughed. Then she shrugged her shoulders. "Life would be simpler if you could believe in such a thing."

"I don't know," I said. And Eiko said: "More hopeful."

My departure was now so close that it somehow paralyzed me. I had a few last days off, and toured the city with my camera, taking pictures of the places I wanted to remember, my neighborhood, my regular bar, the ferry to Staten Island, and the midtown area where I had worked. But it was as though the city was slipping away from me even while I clicked, as though it were stiffening, flattening, into a photograph, a memory, before my eyes.

All at once I had the feeling of being at home here. At first I couldn't explain why, then I realized that, for the first time since I'd been in New York, I was hearing church bells.

On the day before my departure, it snowed. In the space of a few hours, a thick blanket of snow covered the city. The radio was full of news of closed subway lines, and jams on the main exit roads. There were reports of flooding in Monmouth and Far Rockaway. Chris, who had gone to a party with Eiko, called to say they would have to stay the night there, and so wouldn't be able to say goodbye to me.

"I'll visit you," I said.

"Sure," said Chris. "Good luck."

I had packed my bags, and was watching TV to kill the time. Every station had reports on the flooding and the snow. Eventually I sat down in the window once more, and smoked. There was no light on in the dancer's window, nor in Margarita's either. Down on the street, some kids were playing in the snow. I watched them, and thought about my own childhood, and how we used to play in the snow. I felt happy to be going back to Switzerland.

Then one of the kids spotted me, and lobbed a snowball up in my direction. The others all looked up as well. They interrupted their game, and now all of them were throwing snowballs at me. It was too high up for them, but one of the snowballs hit just below me, and some of the snow splattered in my face. I shut the window, and took a step back into the shade. The children went back to whatever game they had been playing before. They seemed to have already forgotten all about me.

BLACK ICE

I was amazed to see how small a heart was. It was lying in the patient's opened chest, beating quickly and regularly. The ribs were pinned back by two metal clamps. The surgeon had had to cut through a thick layer of fat, and I was surprised that the wound wasn't bleeding. The operation took two hours, and then the green cloths surrounding the patient were taken away. In front of us was an old man lying naked on the operating table. One of his legs had been amputated above the knee, and he had three large scars on his belly, from previous operations. His arms were spread wide, and tied down, as if he wanted to embrace someone. I turned away.

"Was it interesting for you?" asked the surgeon as we drank coffee together later.

"A heart's such a small thing," I said. "I think I'd rather not have seen that."

"It's small, but it's tough," he said. "Originally, I was going to go into psychiatry."

I had come to the clinic to write up the case of a young woman patient. She had tuberculosis, and, in the course of her treatment at a different lung clinic, had contracted an incurable form of the illness.

At first, the patient had agreed to be interviewed, but when I came to the clinic she changed her mind. I waited two days, walked in the park, looked up at her window, and hoped she would agree to see me. On the second day, the consultant asked me whether I'd like to see an operation, to shorten my waiting time. On the morning of the third day, the tuberculosis specialist called me in the hotel, and said his patient would see me now.

The TB ward was in an old, separate building. There was no one to be seen on the large, glazed balconies. There were Christmas decorations up in the windows and the corridors inside. I read the information on the notice board, the business card of a hairdresser who did home visits, television rental offers. A nurse helped me into green scrubs that buttoned at the back, and handed me a mask.

"Larissa isn't actually infectious," she said, "as long as she doesn't cough in your face. But it's best to be safe."

"I would like to talk to you as well," I said, "if you have any time on any of the next few evenings . . ."

Larissa was sitting on her bed. I wanted to shake hands, hesitated, and ending up just saying hello. I sat down. Larissa was pale, and very thin. Her eyes were dark and she had unkempt thick dark hair. She was wearing a tracksuit and pink fluffy slippers.

We didn't talk very long on our first meeting. Larissa said she was tired, and feeling unwell. When I told her about myself and the magazine I was working for, it seemed hardly to interest her. She no longer read much, she said. To begin with, she had, but not anymore. She showed me a doll without a face and just one arm.

"She's for my daughter, a Christmas present. I wanted to give it to her on her birthday, but I couldn't get it together. I feel like knitting, but instead I watch television, or the doctor comes, or it's mealtime. And the evening comes, and I've gotten no further. And every day is like that, and every week, and every month."

"She's pretty," I said.

The doll was ghastly. Larissa took it out of my hands, hugged it, and said: "I can only knit when I've got company. If I have company, then I can knit."

Then she said she wanted to watch a film with Grace Kelly and Alec Guinness. She had seen it the day before, on a different channel. Grace Kelly played a princess who was in love with the Crown Prince. To make him jealous, she pretended to be in love with her tutor. And the tutor had been in love with her for a long time.

"The professor says to her, you're like a mirage. He says you see a beautiful-looking picture in front of you and you rush toward it, but then it vanishes and you'll never, ever see it again. And then she falls in love with him, and kisses him on the mouth. Just once. But the priest—he's an uncle of hers—he says, if you think you're happy, then your happiness is already over. And in the end she marries the Crown Prince. And the professor leaves. Because he says you're like a swan. Always on the lake, majestic and cool. But you'll never come ashore. Because if a swan comes ashore, it looks like a silly goose. To be a bird and never to fly, he says, to dream of a song but never be able to sing it."

The clinic was some way out of the city, in the middle of the industrial park, right on the highway. I had taken a room in a hotel in the vicinity, an ugly new construction in rustic style. So far the only time I had seen the other occupants had been at breakfast time; most of them seemed to be sales reps. Later on, while I was reading the paper, a couple walked into the dining room. She was much younger than him, and he seemed so besotted with her I assumed he must be married, and she was his lover, or else a prostitute.

The hotel had a sauna in the basement, and that evening I put the fifteen marks on my bill, and went down. I found myself in a large, unheated room, empty except for a couple of exercise machines, and a ping pong table. "Roman Baths," it said on a door. Inside, there was soft music coming from loudspeakers in the ceiling. The walls and floor were covered with white tiles. There was no one else around. I sat down in the sauna cabin. I sweated, but then, as soon as I went out to take a shower, I shivered.

The following day I went out to see Larissa again. She said she was feeling better. I asked her to tell me something about herself, and she talked about her family, her home in Kazakhstan, the desert there, and her life. I avoided asking her any questions about her illness, but eventually she got onto the subject herself. After a couple of hours, she said she was tired. I asked if I might come again the next day, and she said yes.

Before I left the room, I looked around and wrote down: "A table, two chairs, a bed, a washbasin behind a yellow flowered plastic screen, everywhere used paper tissues, pictures of her daughter on the wall, and a chocolate Advent calendar, empty. The TV on throughout. Sound off." Larissa looked at me questioningly.

"Atmosphere," I said.

When I got back to the hotel, the photographer had arrived. I had made a date for that evening with Gudrun, the nurse on the TB ward. I called her to ask if she had a colleague she could bring along. The four of us ate in a Greek restaurant, the photographer and I, and the two nurses, Gudrun and Yvonne.

"How long have you been smoking?" Yvonne asked me, as I lit up after supper.

"Ten years," I said. She asked me how many I smoked, and together we toted up the number of cigarettes I had smoked in my life.

"Well, it's still better than TB," I said.

"TB is no problem," said Yvonne. "You can be cured in six months. And it heightens desire. Your sex drive."

"Is that really true?"

"It's what they say. Maybe it just used to. In the days when people still used to die of it. A kind of terminal panic."

"He's writing about Larissa," said Gudrun.

"That's a bad case," said Yvonne, shaking her head.

I liked Yvonne better than Gudrun, who seemed to prefer the photographer. Once, I winked at him, and he laughed and winked back.

"What are you doing, winking at each other?" said Gudrun, laughing as well.

When I went in to Larissa the next day, with the photographer in tow, she insisted on getting changed. She pulled the yellow curtain rather carelessly, and I saw her pale, emaciated body, and thought she must have gotten used to changing behind curtains. I turned away and went up to the window.

When Larissa came out from behind the curtains, she was wearing jeans, a loud patterned sweater, and black patent leather pumps. She said we could go out on the balcony, but the photographer said the room was better.

"Atmosphere," he explained.

I could see him sweating under his mask. Larissa smiled as he took her picture.

"He's a good-looking man," she said, after the photographer was gone.

"All photographers are good-looking," I said. "People only want to have their picture taken by good-looking people."

"The doctors are good-looking as well," said Larissa, "and healthy too. They never get sick."

I told her about the high suicide rate among doctors, but she refused to believe me.

"That's something I would never do," she said, "take my life."

"Do you know how much longer . . ."

"Half a year, nine months maybe . . ."

"Can't they do anything?"

"No," said Larissa, and she laughed hoarsely, "it's spread all over my body. All rotten."

She talked about her first spell in a clinic, and how she had left thinking she was cured. Then she had become pregnant, and had got married.

"I would never have dared before. And when I was in the hospital for the birth, that's when it all began again. Slowly. They treated me at home for six months, and then they said it was too dangerous. For my baby. I was so afraid, so afraid they might catch it from me. But they're healthy. Thank God. They're both healthy. I was still living at home this Easter. My husband cooked. And he said, in six months the doctor said you'll be better. By the time Sabrina has her first birthday, in October, you'll be home again. In May, on my birthday, he came with a ring."

She slid off the ring she had on her finger. She held it in her fist, and said: "We had no money before, we bought furniture, a television, things for Sabrina. The ring wasn't a priority, we told each other. In May he brought me the ring. Now we need it, he said."

Then Larissa said she wanted to see my face. She tied on a mask, and I took mine off. She looked at me for a long time in silence, and only then did I notice her beautiful eyes. Finally she said, all right, and I tied my mask back on.

That evening we went to the sauna with the two nurses. When the photographer suggested it, Gudrun giggled, but Yvonne agreed straight off. I hardly broke a sweat during the first session, and remained sitting long after the sand timer was empty. The photographer and Gudrun had left in quick succession.

"Shall I pour on more water?" Yvonne asked, and, without waiting for my agreement, poured water on the heated stones. There was a hiss, and a smell of peppermint. We sat facing each other in the dim sauna. In the low lighting, Yvonne's body glistened with sweat, and I thought she was beautiful.

"Don't these mixed saunas bother you?" I asked.

"Why?" she asked. She said she belonged to a gym, and often used saunas.

"I don't like it," I said. "Being naked, as though it didn't signify anything. We're not wild beasts."

"Then why did you agree to come?"

"There's nothing else to do here."

As we finally left, Gudrun and the photographer were just returning. And from then on, we took turns. While we rested, they sweated, while we sweated, they rested and showered. I lay next to Yvonne on one bench. I turned to the side, and watched her. She was flipping through a car journal, whose pages had gotten dulled and wavy with the moisture.

"Somehow I can't reason myself out of it," I said, "a naked woman is a naked woman."

"Are you married?" she asked rather indifferently, without looking up from her magazine.

"I live with my girlfriend," I said. "What about you?"

She shook her head.

After three goes, we had had enough. When Yvonne got dressed, she seemed more naked to me than she had in the sauna. Then we played ping pong, and the photographer and Gudrun sat down on the exercise machines to watch. Finally, Gudrun said she was getting cold, and the two of them went upstairs to the bar. Yvonne was a good player, and beat me. I asked her for a rematch, and she beat me again. We had built up a sweat, and so we had another shower.

"Shall we have a drink?" Yvonne asked.

"Men are so straightforward," I said, and I had the feeling my voice was trembling.

"How do you mean?" she asked, coolly doing up her shoes.

"I don't know," I said. And then I asked her: "Will you come upstairs with me?"

"No," she said, and looked at me with disbelief, "absolutely not. What's going on?"

I said I was sorry, but she just turned and walked off. I followed her upstairs to the bar.

"Are you coming?" she said to Gudrun. "I want to go home."

When the two of them had gone, the photographer asked me what had happened. I told him I had asked Yvonne to come upstairs with me. He said I was a fool.

"Did you fall in love with her?"

"I don't know. How should I know? What are we doing here?"

"So long as you don't fall in love with your beautiful patient."

"Do you think so?"

"Yes, she's got something. But don't expect a writer to see that."

He laughed, threw his arm around me, and said: "Come on, let's have another beer. We can enjoy our evening even without those two."

The following morning, the photographer left. The nurses on the TB ward were less friendly than they'd been before. I didn't see Yvonne, but I assumed she'd talked. I didn't care.

"How many more times do you plan on coming?" asked the head sister.

"Till I have enough material," I said.

"I hope you're not taking advantage of your situation."

"What do you mean by that?"

"Frau Lehman has been in isolation for the past six months. She is very receptive to any kind of attention. If she experienced a disappointment, it might affect her adversely."

"Does she not get any visitors?"

"No," said the ward sister, "her husband's stopped coming."

Larissa was wearing her jeans again. She had combed her hair, and was wearing make-up. I looked at her, and thought the photographer was right.

"That's the worst thing," said Larissa, "the fact that no one ever touches me. Not for six months now. Except in rubber gloves. I haven't kissed anyone in six months. I sensed . . . when my husband brought me here, I sensed he was scared of me. He kissed me on the cheek, and said in six months . . . It was as though that was the moment that I got sick. The night before we slept together. That was the last time. Though I didn't know that then. And when we arrived here, he was suddenly afraid of me. I can still picture him shaving in his shorts, while I'm packing up my toilet articles. And he says to me, take the toothpaste with you, I'll buy a new tube. And I took it."

She said she sometimes kissed her hand, her arm, the pillow, the chair. I didn't say anything. I didn't know what to say. Larissa lay down and cried. I went up to her bed, and put my hand on her head. She sat up and said: "You must disinfect your hand."

I had enough material for my story. That evening, I went downtown for supper. But I couldn't stand the racket, and soon took the bus out to the industrial park. As I got out at the terminus, I thought of Larissa. She told me she had tried running away one evening. When a nurse had forgotten to lock her room. She had gone as far as the bus stop. She had stood a little separately, and watched the people arriving from the factory. They must have imagined she too had come from there. Was on her way home. Would pop into a store on the way, and get home and fix dinner for her husband and child. That they would watch television together afterwards. And then she had gone back to the clinic.

It was still early. I walked through the industrial park. In among the ugly factories were a few new homes. They were dwarfed by the structures around them, as if they had been built to a different scale. Outside one of the homes, a man was hanging electric lights on a tree. In the doorway, a woman and a little child stood and watched him. The woman was smoking. A man in an apron was setting the table. I wondered whether he was expecting guests, or if he was cooking for himself or for his family. In the distance, I could hear the traffic on the highway. Then I went back to the hotel. It had gotten cold. Yvonne was sitting at the bar. I sat down next to her and ordered a beer. For a while we didn't speak, and then finally I said: "Do you come here often?"

"I've come to see you," she said.

I said I hadn't meant it unpleasantly.

She said: "I'm not like that."

"I'm not either. I don't know what's the matter with me. All those sick people . . . I had the feeling that nothing that happened here counted. That everything was excused. And that we had to hurry. Because there's not much time."

Yvonne said we could go back to her place, if I liked. She said she lived in a village a few miles from here. Her car was parked outside.

Yvonne drove far too fast. "You'll kill us both," I said.

She laughed and said: "My car is my favorite thing. It spells freedom for me."

The furniture in Yvonne's apartment was all chrome and glass. There were some red weights in a corner. In the hall there was a little cheap frame, with a piece of paper in it that said: "You can get it if you really want it."

"It's cold in your place," I said.

"Yes," said Yvonne, "I expect that's the way I like it."

"Do you believe that," I asked, "that you can get it if you really want it?"

"No," said Yvonne, "though I'd like to. What about you?"

"I didn't get you."

"You don't 'get' people," she said. "If you really wanted . . . And if you were patient . . ."

I said I didn't have much time. Yvonne went into the kitchen, and I followed her.

"Water, orange juice, wheat grass, or tea?" she asked.

We drank tea, and Yvonne told me about her job, and why she had gone into nursing. I asked what she did in her time off, and she said she was into fitness. In the evenings, she was usually too tired to go out. On the weekends, she visited her parents.

"I'm all right," she said, "I'm doing fine."

Then she took me back to the hotel. She kissed me on the cheek.

In the morning, it was snowing gently. The puddles on the way to the clinic were frozen. In the newspaper I read that there had been four fatal accidents on the roads that night. "Black ice," the headlines said.

Larissa was already waiting for me. She told me about a film she had seen the night before. Then we were silent for a long time. Finally, she said she would die of increasing weakness, when her weight loss got to be too great. Or of a hemorrhage. That meant coughing up blood, not a lot, a small glass of it. It didn't hurt, but it happened quickly, in a few minutes. And it could happen quite suddenly.

"What are you telling me that for?"

"I thought you were interested. Isn't that what you're here for?"

"I don't know," I said, "maybe you're right."

"I can't talk to anyone here," Larissa said. "They don't tell me the truth."

Then she looked down and said: "Desire never stops. No matter how weak I am. At first, when I was with my husband, we made love every single day. Sometimes . . . once in a forest. We went for a walk. It was damp in the forest, it smelled of earth. We did it standing up, against a tree. Thomas was worried in case someone saw us."

Larissa went up to the window and looked out. She hesitated, and then she said: "Here, I do it for myself. At night, only ever at night. Do you do that? Because I can imagine . . . and because . . . and because the nurses don't knock before they come in . . . Desire never stops."

And then she fell silent. There was a documentary on the natural world on television. The sound was off. I saw a herd of antelope gallop silently over a plain.

"The old films will be on again soon. Christmastime, you know," I said.

"This will be my first Christmas in the clinic," said Larissa, "and my last."

When I left the ward, I ran into Yvonne in the corridor. She smiled and asked me: "What are you doing tonight?"

I said I would have to work.

I crossed the hospital grounds. For the first time, I was struck by the many faces in the windows. And I was struck by the way the visitors walked faster than the patients. A few were crying, and their heads were down, and I hoped I wouldn't feel ashamed if it was ever my turn to mourn for someone. The mini golf course beside the hospital was littered with fallen leaves. There were deer in the forest, Larissa had told me. And squirrels. And she fed the birds from her balcony.

As evening fell, I was walking through the industrial park again. I bought a hamburger at a fast-food joint. I came to a vast building, a furniture warehouse, and went in. In the entry hall were dozens of deckchairs; dozens of TV lounges had been simulated. I walked through the series of model lives, and was surprised at how much they all resembled each other. I tried to imagine this or that item in my apartment. And then I thought of Larissa, and I wondered which easy chair she and her husband had bought. And I thought of her husband, who was sitting in their apartment all alone, maybe drinking a beer, maybe thinking of Larissa. And I thought of their little girl, whose name I couldn't just now remember. I thought she was probably asleep now anyway.

Beside the exit to the superstore, there were Christmas decorations in big baskets, chains of lights, illuminated plastic snowmen, and small crudely carved cribs. "We look forward to your visit, Monday to Friday, 10 A.M. — 8 P.M., Saturdays, 10 A.M. — 4 P.M.," I read on the glass door, as I left the store. Darkness had fallen.

The next day was my last. I looked in on Larissa to say goodbye. Once again, she started telling me about her childhood in Kazakhstan, the desert, and her grandfather, her father's father, who had gone east from Germany.

"When he was dying, the priest came. And they talked together for a while. He was old. And then the priest asked him, well, Anton—my grandfather's name was Anton— what sort of life did you have? And do you know what my grandfather said? It was cold, he said, all my life I was cold. Even though it got so hot in the summer. He said, my whole life, I was cold. He never got used to the desert."

She laughed, and then she said: "It passes so quickly. Sometimes I switch the television off, so that it doesn't pass quite so quickly. But then I find it even harder to stand."

She talked about one of her neighbors in Kazakhstan, whose television screen was broken, but who kept switching it on anyway and staring at the black screen.

"Just as you look out the window when it's dark, because you know there's something there. Even if you can't see anything," she said. "I'm scared. And fear won't leave me. Not till the very end."

She said fear was like losing your balance. The way that, before you fell, you had a momentary feeling of being torn into pieces, of bursting open, in all directions. And sometimes it was like hunger, or like suffocating, and sometimes like being squashed. Larissa spoke fast, and I had a sense she wanted to tell me everything she had thought in the last few months. As though she wanted me to be a witness, tell me her whole life for me to write down.

I got up and said goodbye to her. She asked if I would come to her funeral, and I said no, I probably wouldn't. When I turned around in the door, she was watching television. I went home that afternoon.

Two weeks later, I sent Larissa some chocolate. I didn't send her copies of the photographs. She looked too ill in them. She didn't write. Yvonne sent me a couple of friendly letters, but I never replied.

I came back from another assignment six months ago, and found a death notice in my mailbox. The chief consultant had written "with best wishes" at the bottom of it.

IN STRANGE GARDENS

He looked out of the window into a strange garden,
and saw many people standing together,
some of whom he recognized straight away.

—Johann Wolfgang von Goethe
Wilhelm Meister's Apprenticeship, Book VII

THE VISIT

The house was too big. The children had managed to fill it, but ever since Regina was living in it on her own, it had begun to grow. Successively she had withdrawn from the rooms; one after another they had become strange to her, and she had finally given them up.

After the children had moved out, she and Gerhard had spread themselves out in it a little. Previously, they had had the smallest room for themselves, now at last there was space for everything, a study, a sewing room, a guest bedroom, where the children would stay when they came to visit, or the grandchildren. But there was only one grandchild. Martina was born to Verena, who had married a carpenter in the next village. When Martina had been a little baby, Regina had minded her a few times. But Verena had always insisted that her mother come to her. Nor did Regina's other children, Otmar and Patrick, ever stay the night. They preferred to drive back to the city late at night. Why don't you stay the night here, Regina would always say, but her sons needed to be at work early the next day, or they found some other reason why they had to go.

At first, the children had had keys to the house. Regina had almost forced them each to have a copy of the big old key. She thought it was the natural thing. But over the years, one of them after the other had handed back their key. They were afraid of losing it, they said, they could ring the bell, after all their mother was always at home. And what if anything were to happen? Well, then they knew where the cellar key was hidden.

Once, though, the children did stay overnight, all three of them, and that was when Gerhard was dying. Regina had phoned them, and they came as quickly as they could. They arrived in the hospital and stood around the bed, and didn't know what to do or say. At night they took turns, and whoever wasn't in the hospital was in the house. Regina made up the beds, and apologized to the children because the sewing machine was in Verena's room, and Otmar had the big desk that Gerhard had been able to buy cheap when his company invested in a new set of office furniture.

Regina had lain down to get some rest, but she was unable to sleep. She heard the children talking among themselves quietly in the kitchen. In the morning, they all went to the hospital together. Verena kept looking at her watch, and Otmar, the eldest, was on his mobile telephone the whole time, canceling or postponing appointments. At around noon, Gerhard died, and Regina and the children went home, and did whatever needed to be done. But that very evening, they all drove off. Verena had asked if everything was okay, whether her mother could manage, and she promised to come early the next morning. Regina watched her children go, and saw them talking to each other in front of the house. She knew what they were talking about.

After her husband's death, the house was even emptier. Regina no longer opened the bedroom shutters in the daytime, as though she was afraid of the light. She got up, washed, and made coffee. She went down to the mailbox, and picked up the paper. She didn't set foot in the bedroom all day. Eventually, she thought she would only occupy the living room and kitchen, and treat the other rooms as though they had strangers living in them. Then she wondered what had been the point of buying the house in the first place. The years had gone by, the children were living in their own houses, which they furnished according to their own tastes, and which were more practical and more lived in. But even these houses would one day fall empty.

There was a little birdbath in the garden, and during the winter Regina would feed the birds, long before there was any snow on the ground. She hung little balls of suet in the Japanese maple that stood in front of the house. One especially cold winter the tree froze, and the next spring it didn't bud anymore and had to be chopped down. On summer nights Regina left the upstairs windows open, and hoped a bird or bat might err into the house, and maybe make its nest there.

When there was a birthday to be celebrated, Regina invited the children to the house, and sometimes they were all free, and could all come. Regina cooked lunch, and washed up in the kitchen. She made coffee. When she went upstairs to fetch a fresh pack of coffee, the children would all be standing in their former rooms like visitors to a museum, shy or inattentive. They leaned against the furniture or perched on the windowsills and talked about politics, or their jobs, or where they had gone on vacation. Over lunch, Regina would always try to steer the conversation round to their father, but the children avoided the topic, and in the end she gave up as well.

This Christmas, for the first time, Verena hadn't come back to the house. She was spending the holiday in the mountains with her husband and Martina, where her in-laws had a vacation house. As ever, Regina had hidden the presents in the wardrobe in her bedroom, as though it could never occur to anyone to go looking for them. She prepared Christmas lunch. She emptied the leftovers onto the compost heap, where a little snow still lay. A week before it had snowed, and it had remained cold since, and yet most of the snow had melted. Regina tried to remember the last time there had been a white Christmas. Then she went back in the house and turned on the radio. There was Christmas music on every single station. Regina stood by the window. She hadn't turned on a light. She looked across at the neighbors' house. When she did finally switch on the light, it gave her a shock, and she quickly turned it off again.

The whole family came for Regina's seventy-fifth birthday. She had invited them all to a restaurant. The food was good, it was a fine occasion. Otmar and his girlfriend were the first to go, Patrick left shortly afterwards, and then Verena and her husband said goodbye. Martina had brought along her boyfriend, an Australian who was an exchange student at the school for a year. She said she didn't feel like going home yet. There was an argument, and then Regina said why didn't Martina spend the night in her house. What about her friend? There were more than enough rooms, said Regina. She saw Verena and her husband to the gate. "Make sure she doesn't get up to any nonsense," said Verena.

Regina went back to the restaurant, and paid the bill. She asked Martina whether she wanted to go out anywhere still with her friend, she could easily give her a key. But Martina shook her head, and her friend smiled.

They walked back, the three of them. The Australian boy was called Philip. He spoke hardly any German, and it was many years since Regina had last tried speaking English. As a young woman she had spent a year in England, just after the end of the war, had stayed with a family and looked after the children. It had felt to her at the time as though she had just come into the world. She got acquainted with a young Englishman, went out to concerts and pubs with him on her evenings off, and kissed him on the way home. Perhaps she should have stayed in England. When she returned to Switzerland, everything was different.

Regina unlocked the door, and turned on lights. "This is a nice house," said Philip, and he took off his shoes. Martina disappeared into the bathroom to shower. Regina brought in a towel for her. Through the frosted glass of the shower cabinet, she could see Martina's slim body, her head tipped back, the long dark hair.

Regina went into the kitchen. The Australian had sat down at the table. He had a tiny computer on his knees. She asked him if she could get him something. "Do you want a drink?" she said. It sounded like a line out of a film. The Australian smiled and said something back to her that she didn't understand. He motioned to her to come closer, and pointed to the screen of his computer. Regina went over to him and saw an aerial photograph of a town. The Australian pointed to a spot on the picture. Regina didn't understand what he was saying, but she knew that that was where he lived, and where he would return, once the year here was over. "Yes," she said, "yes, nice," and she smiled. The Australian pressed a button, and the town receded, you saw the land and the sea, the whole of Australia, and finally the whole world. He looked at Regina with a triumphant smile, and she felt much closer to him than to her own granddaughter. She wanted to feel closer to him, because he would leave Martina, just as Gerhard had left her. This time she wanted to be on the side of the strong, on the side of the ones who went.

Regina made up the bed in Otmar's room. Martina was upstairs. She had got dressed again.

"Can I lend you some pajamas?" Regina asked.

"We can share a bed," said Martina, seeing Regina hesitating. "You don't have to tell Mom."

She put her arm around her grandmother, and kissed her on the cheek. Regina looked at her granddaughter. She said nothing. Martina followed her downstairs and into the kitchen, where Philip was typing something on his computer. Martina stood behind his chair, and laid her hands on his shoulders. She said something to him in English.

"You're very good at that," said Regina. Martina struck her as being very grown up at that moment, perhaps for the first time, more grown up than she was herself, full of the strength and poise that women need. Regina said goodnight, she was going to bed. And then Martina and Philip sat in her kitchen, as if it were theirs, as if the house were theirs. But that didn't upset Regina. For the first time in a long time, she had the sense of the house being full again. She thought about Australia, where she had never been. She thought of the aerial photograph that Philip had showed her, and then she thought of Spain, where she had been on vacation a couple of times, with the children. Regina stood in the bathroom, brushing her teeth. She was tired. When she went out on the landing and saw a little beam of light under the kitchen door, she was glad that Martina and Philip were still up.

Regina lay in bed. She heard Philip go to the bathroom and shower. She wanted to get up again, and bring him a towel, but then she let it go. She imagined him stepping out of the shower, drying himself on Martina's damp towel, walking down the hall to the kitchen, where Martina was waiting for him. They would embrace, go upstairs, and then go to bed together. Verena had asked her to see that there was no nonsense between them. But it wasn't nonsense. Everything flashed by so quickly.

Regina got up once more, and stepped into the landing without turning on the light. She stood in the dark, and listened. There was no sound. She went into the bathroom. The streetlamp outside shed a bit of light in the room. The towel was lying on the rim of the bathtub. Regina picked it up and buried her face in it. It felt cool against her forehead, and it had an unfamiliar smell. She put it down, and went back to her room.

When she was back in her bed she thought about Australia, where she would never go. She would probably never see Spain again either, she thought, but she was maybe good for one more trip somewhere.

THE WALL OF FIRE

There was only a hiss coming out of the television. Henry turned up the sound as far as it went, and stepped outside. It was still hot. He adjusted the satellite dish, which was mounted on an improvised wooden stand on the asphalt. He knew the rough position of the satellite, southeast. West was where the sun went down. Then the hiss was suddenly gone, and Henry could hear music and voices. He climbed up the metal steps. It was airless in his little cubbyhole behind the driver's cab that he called home. Bed, chair, TV, fridge, everything a man needed. There was no window, but on the walls were a couple of American flags, a Marlboro poster, and a placard for some Erotica Fair that Henry had pulled off a wall somewhere. He turned off the TV, picked up his deckchair, and sat down in front of the truck in the evening sun. The piled up containers cast long shadows.

The caravans of the others were still in the next village, where they had performed yesterday. It had taken them the whole day to get the cars and all the rest of the stuff over here, and to put up the wooden grandstand. At noon

it had rained, but Joe had been in a foul mood even before that. Joe was like that, up and down the whole time.
And Charlie had been God knows where, and Oskar had
been tooling around with his motorbikes. With the result
that once again Henry had done all the work on his own.
Henry the daredevil. Actually he was more like the
nightwatchman, the maid of all work, the odd job man,
the spare prick at the wedding. Only during the shows he
was the fire devil, who lay on the roof of the car as Oskar
drove through the wall of fire.

The others had nice trailers, Joe's you could extend every
which way, it was like a proper apartment with a lounge
unit and a video and all the works. Henry wanted a trailer
like that for himself. And he wanted a woman, too, and a
kid. He wasn't far short of forty now and the boss wouldn't
object, so long as it was the right girl. One like Oskar's
Jackie, or Charlie's Verena, or Joe's Petra, who cooked for
Henry as well, and sometimes washed his clothes. The
others had it all, and he had nothing. But then a woman
set you back more than a new pair of pants.

Henry couldn't complain. He had his peace and quiet,
and he got to see places. In fact, he could hardly do much
better for himself. What did he lack? He was doing fine,
better than in the old GDR. Back then, he'd been a milk-
man. After the Wall came down, he was out of a job. He'd
let them make a monkey of him. He had hung around on
corners, got into scrapes, and went through his little bit
of unemployment benefit in gambling saloons. Then one

evening Joe and his boys had come into town, and after the performance Henry had gone over to the artistes and helped them take down the stand. They could sure use someone like him, Joe had said, and Henry grinned. It wasn't something he often got to hear. Then he joined the troupe, just went along with them when they left town the next day. And ever since then, he'd been traveling with them, from village to village and town to town. He put up his antenna, kept an eye on the cars, and every night crashed head first through the wall of fire.

The fire devil, that had been Petra's idea. Henry the Fire Devil. He'd been with the troupe now for six or seven years, living behind the cab. This year you're getting a trailer, Joe had promised, but then he said he didn't want them to get to look like a bunch of Gypsies, and someone after all had to mind the vehicles at night. Some day, Joe said, you'll find yourself a woman. And then we'll think again. And Oskar promised he would teach Henry how to drive on two wheels.

Henry heard a noise, a quiet thump. He got up and walked over to the cars. The asphalt was still glistening with rain, and as Henry ran through the piled up containers, he felt like an Indian in the Grand Canyon. There was another thump. Henry ran to the cars, just in time to see a stone fly through the air and smash against the rear window of one of the cars. He ran in the direction from which the stone had come. And then he saw the kids running off. He swore, picked a rock off the ground, and flung it at them. But they had already run around the back of the containers.

Henry stood on the tracks, which seemed to go on endlessly in either direction. He looked left and right, and then he set off. On the other side of the embankment, he stopped. He waited for a long time till a goods train came. He counted the cars, just as he had done when he was a kid. In America, there were people who hopped on the goods trains, and traveled the length and breadth of the country. Henry wondered where this train was going. He counted forty-two cars. Gravel.

The sun had dipped behind the nearby line of hills, but it was still light. Henry walked along the embankment till he came to a path, which led to the main street. From afar he could make out the yellow M, and when he was closer, the life-sized plastic clown who was sitting on a bench outside the snack bar, smiling.

Seated at a corner table were three forestry workers. Behind the bar was a young woman. Manuela, he read on her name tag. Henry ordered a burger and a Coke. They didn't serve beer, Manuela had said. One moment.

"Are you from the East?" she asked him as he paid.

From the East, said Henry, and that he was an artiste. Over there, he said, pointing towards the container depot, there would be a show tomorrow. Car stunts. If she liked, he could get her in for free. Cars, said Manuela, cars didn't really interest her. A stunt show, said Henry, cars driving on two wheels, motorbike leaps over forty people.

"Forty people?" asked Manuela.

"Not actually forty people lying there," said Henry. "Earlier, we used to."

On Monday they'd be gone already, he said. They were headed south, for Greece or Italy or someplace.

"Greece is beautiful," he said. "You can go swimming there every day."

He said his name was Henry. Manuela, she said. I know, said Henry, and he pointed to her name tag. Manuela laughed. Was he really a stuntman? Yes, kind of thing, he said. Did she have a boyfriend? Because she could bring him along as well. No, said Manuela. Her accent was sweet. She was sweet altogether.

"Me neither," said Henry. "On the road the whole time."

There was silence for a moment. Then Manuela said, wait. She disappeared and came back and gave Henry a baked apple pie.

"Here you go," she said. "But careful. It's hot."
Henry thanked her.

"If my boss saw me do that," said Manuela, "I'd be out of a job."

"Then you can come along with us," said Henry.

Manuela had to work till midnight. But tomorrow morning she was free, sure. She didn't go to church or anything. There was nothing to do here on Sundays. Small animal show jointly sponsored by the fur sewing association and the ornithological society.

"Do you like that sort of thing? Birds and bunnies?"
"Sure," said Henry. "It's worth a look."

They arranged to meet at the bus stop at nine o'clock tomorrow morning. But he had to be back by noon, said Henry, to get ready for the matinee.

The pet show didn't have much to offer either of them. After fifteen minutes they were done. They sat in the refreshment tent and drank coffee.

"My father used to have a dog," said Henry. "A German shepherd."

"I used to have a hamster," said Manuela.

"What did you like the best?"

"The rabbits. The baby ones."

"See them in their cages," said Henry. "They were shit scared."

He'd liked the birds best, they were so colorful, the budgies and the finches and all the others. One of the breeders had told him the names and the countries they came from, a big man with a face like a bird and a high squeaky voice. That was from some disease he had, said Manuela. "Do you want some cake?" she asked.

"What? A baked apple pie?" Henry grinned.

"If my boss had caught me," said Manuela.

Then they were quiet for a time. There was a folk music tape playing in the refreshment tent.

"Do you know any jokes?" asked Henry. "D'you like the music?"

"I like Elvis," said Manuela. "Used to. Still do, really."

They drank their coffee and went. They headed out of the village in the direction of the container park. They passed through a development with high-rise blocks. This was where Manuela had grown up. A couple of years ago, her parents had moved away. Now she lived in the village with a girlfriend. The path went along beside the railway tracks. Henry plucked a flower that was growing on the embankment, and offered it to Manuela. She said thank you, and giggled.

"Where I live isn't much more than a rabbit stall," said Henry.

He hadn't thought Manuela would go with him. The poster of the Erotica Fair embarrassed him. But it didn't seem to put her out at all. Bachelor pad, she said, and sat down on the unmade bed.

"Do you often have girls up here?"

"I wish," said Henry. "I'm always on the road. Shitty life."

He kissed her, not very skillfully. And when he tried to take her clothes off, Manuela had to help him. Her jeans were so tight that she had to lie down, while he tugged at the cuffs. Her bra didn't have a fastening, she just pulled it over her head like a T-shirt. Never seen one of those before, said Henry. The rest Manuela did by herself. Then Henry got undressed, quickly, and with his back to her. He sat down on the bed without turning around, and quickly slid under the thin blanket.

"It's cozy here," said Manuela, when Henry was already dressed again, fixing coffee.

"I don't need anything else," he said. "I've got everything I need here."

The others, his colleagues, all came from long lines of artistes, he said. All except him and Jackie, who was married to Oskar. She had hooked up with them, and gone along, same as he had. That kind of thing went on sometimes. She had a husband and three kids. And then she'd met Oskar, and run away, and never gone back. Just left her family behind.

"It happens," said Henry.

"I guess," said Manuela.

The others had done high wire acts before, Henry said. But there weren't the audiences for those anymore. And then Oskar's brother had had a fall. The rope broke. Verena's first husband had fallen off as well. With his motorbike. Henry talked about the accidents, as if he knew the dead people and was proud of them.

"Horrible," said Manuela, and drank her coffee.

"That was in Chemnitz," said Henry.

What did he do in the performance, asked Manuela. He did everything, he said, he was just a sort of odd-job man. And then he explained his number to her.

"You're mad," said Manuela.

"No," said Henry, "not really."

He talked her through the whole thing again. How Oskar accelerated, and he lay on the roof, holding on with his hands and feet. He looked up, saw the wall of fire directly ahead of him. Kept looking, as long as he could. And then: gritted teeth, and head down. He hears the board splinter before he feels the impact. The car crashes through the planks at the bottom. There's a smell of gasoline. The boards shatter, the burning fragments fly through the air. It's like . . .

"It's the greatest feeling."

"You're mad," said Manuela.

"Don't you get it," said Henry. "It's like . . ."

"Doesn't it hurt?" asked Manuela. "You're mad. I've got to go."

It was almost twelve. Henry was glad Manuela was going, he didn't want the others to see her. She promised to come to the evening show. Henry said he would meet her at the entrance. She was to wait for him there, on the left-hand side. Then he would take her in, and she wouldn't have to pay any admission.

"I'll meet you there," he said.

When Manuela was gone, Henry tore down the poster of the Erotica Fair, and made the bed. He wondered what else he could do to make a woman feel at home in the cubbyhole. Manuela had said it was cozy. Perhaps she was like Jackie. Perhaps she just wanted to get away from here, and didn't much care how. The bed wasn't very wide, but it would do for the moment.

Joe was moaning because the kids had smashed a couple of windshields. Hadn't Henry been doing his job. He couldn't be everywhere at once, said Henry. Together they prepared the cars for the afternoon show, tied the doors shut and fixed tires on the roof of the car that Oskar would turn over in. One tire on the Toyota that Henry went through the wall of fire on was completely bald. I really need to watch out here, said Henry. But the rim on the replacement didn't fit, and he put the old tire back on.

"Well, whatever," he said. "If it bursts, it bursts."

Then Charlie turned up with the articulated truck, bringing the two scrap cars that would be crushed later, a Passat and an Alpha Spider. I used to have an Alpha like that, said Charlie, as they unloaded the cars. Oskar revved up the engine of his Kawasaki, and took a couple of turns around the arena. He was always nervous before a show. The first of the spectators were already standing around by the entrance. Petra turned on the P.A. Rock music boomed out of a couple of enormous speakers, and then Petra's voice.

"You will see cars and bikes flying through the air. Things you only thought you'd ever see in films and TV will pass before your eyes . . ."

Slowly the grandstand filled up. A few kids, who could only afford standing seats, clambered up onto the tractor-trucks. It was hot. Henry disappeared into his cubbyhole to put on his blue overalls and get his helmet. He must have crashed through the wall of fire a hundred times, but he still looked forward to his turn every time. The appearance of Henry the Fire Devil.

"It's no good if you don't applaud," he heard Petra's voice over the PA, as he climbed down the steps. Oskar on his bike was flying off the ramp. He flew over what was claimed to be twenty, thirty, forty persons. Then Joe and Charlie in their cars drove around in circles on two wheels, and waved out the windows. The spectators gave them some half-hearted applause.

"That was nothing," Petra said. "Things are going to get really hot around here."

Henry had put up the plank wall, and splashed gasoline over it. He lit it, and ran back to the car, which Oskar had already started up. He climbed onto the roof. The windows were down, so that he could reach inside and get a better grip. He spread his legs. Oskar moved off, accelerated, the wall got nearer. Tonight, thought Henry, I will go through the wall for Manuela. He would give her a sign, or wave, or do something he had never done before. I'll keep my eyes open all the way through, he thought. For Manuela. And maybe she would come back to his van when it was all over and everything was tidied away, and the others were gone.

He never heard the tire burst. He only felt, suddenly, the car seem to stagger and turn aside. Henry's legs lifted off the roof, his belly, he had the feeling his hands were being torn away. Then he let go, and became completely airborne. He was flying, and he saw the astonished faces of the spectators, and he was astonished himself. It was as though the earth below him had come to a stop, as though only he were moving. Henry flew through the air, he flew ever higher and farther. It was lovely. He saw the blue heaven above him, and there were a couple of dark clouds too that had gathered. Maybe it was going to rain.

Manuela spent the afternoon at the gravel-pit with her friend Denise. She had shown her the bite-mark Henry had left on her neck.

"How old is he?" Denise asked, and they both laughed.

"He's sweet," said Manuela. "An Ossi."

"What kind of name is Henry," said Denise. "Honestly, I don't know where you get them from."

"He's a stuntman," said Manuela. "He was so sweet. He can't have done it much. Certainly didn't feel like he had."

"I'm going in the water," said Denise. "Are you coming?"

But Manuela didn't like the water. She lay in the sun, and her body kept getting heavier and warmer. She felt the sun burning on her skin, and when she pressed her ear to the ground, she heard the dull echo of footsteps. She thought of the summer just begun, the long summer ahead, the many evenings she would spend at the gravel pit with Denise and her other friends. She thought of the fires they would light, and the boys who drove too fast in their souped-up cars when they went somewhere after bathing, maybe the Domino, or the town, or just the bar behind the station. She would have liked so much to fall in love with one of the boys, but they were all such babies. Last summer, she had gone out with Andi. It was Andi who had the kiosk at the gravel-pit, and didn't do badly out of it. In the winter he didn't do anything, by lunchtime he'd be in the pub, chatting up the Yugoslav waitress. You've got to make up your mind, she said to him. In the end, it was she who had decided. They had known each other from their school days.

Manuela thought about what it might be like to be on the road with the artistes. But she didn't feel like living with Henry in that dirty cubby hole, with no bath or anything. It felt hot in that tiny space, and there was a smell of dirty clothes and reheated meals. And she didn't know the others. Jackie, who had left her family. And the rest of them she barely even knew the names of. Funny names, too. Manuela tried to picture herself hanging up laundry outside a caravan, and she wondered where the kids would go to school, if you spent the whole time on the road going from town to town. In Greece, too. She had been to Greece once, one summer, with her parents. It was incredibly hot, stiflingly hot, and she hadn't understood a word. When he gave her the flower, that was nice. But Henry had to be ten years older than she was. I'm still young, she thought, I'm not going to fall for that.

"He lies on top of a car, and the car smashes through a wall of fire," she said when Denise came back, and shook out her wet hair. "Ooh, stop it!"

"I've never heard of anything as crazy as that," said Denise. "I'm sure there's a trick somewhere. Like there is in films. What time is it?"

"Three thirty," said Denise. "It's no trick. He actually does it."

Clouds had gathered, and Manuela and Denise had sat up and put on their T-shirts.

At five there was a brief shower of rain. The two women ran to the kiosk for shelter. They chatted to Andi a bit.

He gave them each an ice cream, and asked them if they were going to the Domino tonight. There was a band playing from the next village.

"We're going to the stunt show," said Manuela, "you know, at the container depot."

"She's fallen for a stuntman," said Denise.

"Rubbish," said Manuela. "Maybe afterwards."

When the rain eased, it was no cooler, if anything it was even more oppressive. The wet containers glistened in the flat sunlight. Denise had accompanied Manuela to the show. She was curious to get a glimpse of Henry. But Henry wasn't there.

"He's forgotten all about you," said Denise.

"I don't believe that," said Manuela.

As the show was about to start, they went up to the fat woman who was selling the tickets, and bought a couple.

At the end of the show, a pickup with huge tires crushed the junk cars that two of the artistes had pushed onto the arena. That was the high point of the show, the fat lady had told them.

"Which one is him?" asked Denise, but Manuela just shook her head.

"What do we do now?" said Denise.

At last the pickup came to a stop on top of one of the flattened cars, and the driver climbed out of the cab, clambered down a little ladder, and jumped out onto the arena. The spectators applauded.

"All things must pass," said the woman on the PA and turned off the music. The spectators got to their feet. A few of them gathered round the squashed cars that were lying there like dead animals. A couple of kids tugged at their battered doors, and kicked out at the wheels. A man tried to tear away the Alfa sign. "You couldn't have lined up forty people in that space," he said. "No way."

The artistes were off to one side, talking among themselves. Manuela thought they looked disappointed about something. Sad, even. Gradually the spectators drifted away. From out in front she could hear the roar of engines, and tire screech. Manuela and Denise sat all alone on the grandstand. They watched the men clear up. A few youths from the village helped.

Denise asked: "Shall we go?"

"The one with the wall of fire, he was someone else," said Manuela.

"He must have been lying to you," said Denise.

"But it wasn't a trick. I'm sure it was for real."

Then the artistes started taking down the grandstand, and the women got up to go.

"Maybe he'll turn up still," said Manuela.

"Why don't you ask," said Denise. But Manuela didn't feel like it.

"Shall we go to the Domino?" asked Denise, as they unlocked their bikes.

"Who cares," said Manuela. "It was nothing. Wouldn't have been anything anyway."

IN STRANGE GARDENS

It was summer, and the sun shone through the cracks in the shutters and left little patches of light on the walls of the rooms that were facing the street, narrow stripes, that slowly slid down, and widened when they reached the floor, and crossed the parquet or the carpets, occasionally touching some object or other, a piece of furniture or a stray toy, till the evening, when they climbed up the opposite walls and finally dimmed. The kitchen, whose window shutters were never closed, was bathed in festive light from early in the morning, and if someone had walked in there, he would surely have thought the inhabitants of the house had just stepped out into the garden and would be back at any moment. A cloth was draped over the faucet, as if it had only just been used, and the light struck a half-empty glass of water, where little air bubbles had formed.

The view through the kitchen window was of a garden full of peonies and currant bushes, an old plum tree, and a rather leggy bed of rhubarb. At nine, or a little later but still before it got hot, one might have been able to see the next-door neighbor coming down the gravel path, silently watering the begonias and the herb garden that grew in pots on the kitchen steps. Later on, when she had disappeared behind the house and was filling the big watering cans and watering the tomato plants, the raspberry and blueberry bushes, the rushing of the water sounded unusually loud, the only sound in the silent walls of the house.

She really ought to pick the berries, Ruth had encouraged her; by the time she got back they would be past ripe. But the next-door neighbor didn't pick the berries. She watered the garden every morning, and on the very hottest days she came around a second time in the evening and gave the potted plants another round, and the tomatoes, whose leaves had parched in the heat. When she was finished, she didn't climb over the low fence—which would have been easy enough—she left the garden through the garden gate, and went home along the pavement.

The neighbor had a key to the house, but she didn't like to use it. She unlocked the door and left the mail in the cupboard that was on the porch. She sorted it into two piles, one pile of newspapers and the other of everything else. Through the frosted glass in the inside door, she had a sense of the darkness of the rooms within, and perhaps she saw the shimmer of light that fell through the shutters. She hesitated before opening this second door and going into the kitchen, where Ruth had left all the houseplants. There on the table were fifteen or twenty large and small pots, containing ivy, azaleas, a calla lily with a white flower, and a small ficus. She filled the copper can and watered the plants. She had left the front door and the inner door open. Each time she looked at the half-empty glass next to the sink and thought of rinsing it out, but then finally she didn't, because she thought it might have been left there for a purpose, though she couldn't have said what.

Once, and only once, the next door neighbor went into the sitting room and looked around. On the sideboard there were photographs of the children in little multiple frames, and a few cards. She picked up one of the cards, and read: "Dear Ruth, congratulations on your 40th birthday. We hope you have a wonderful year, bringing you everything you wish for. Love, from Marianne and Beat." The two names had been written in the same hand. The picture was of a mouse with big feet, holding out a bunch of flowers.

It hadn't been a wonderful year for Ruth. I wonder what they've done wrong, the next-door neighbor had often said to her husband, honestly, you would have thought. . . . Nonsense, he had said, without looking up. But it was true: Ruth and her family seemed to have drawn down misfortune upon themselves. Ruth's father had owned the little stationery shop on Main Street. Ruth and her three younger brothers had grown up in the apartment over the shop. Not long after the birth of the third boy, the mother had developed an incurable illness. For a few years, people had watched her hobbling around on a pair of crutches, then one day she stopped leaving the flat, and thereafter she slowly disappeared from their thoughts.

The stationery store doubled as the bookshop. It didn't have much in the way of stock, a single shelf that contained children's books, a few novels, cookbooks, and guide-books to the major cities and to Italy and France. If a cus-tomer wants something different I can always order it, said Ruth's father, who didn't seem to care much about the books. Nor was he often called upon to order anything; most of the people in the town made do with what there was, or else they bought their books in the city. The shop had dark wood paneling, and there was hardly ever any-one in it. Not even the owner seemed to like to spend any time there. If anyone went in, it took a while for him to emerge from a back room, and if they didn't know right away what they wanted to buy, they had to call him back in order to pay.

The three brothers were quiet and serious. They didn't seem to have any friends, though no one had anything to say against them. They didn't attract attention to them-selves, and if they did, then it was more through things happening to them than anything that they did. These lat-ter occurrences, though, were of an odd weight, and some-times of such a violent nature that the whole village talked about them. On one occasion, Elias and Thomas, the two elder boys, had set fire to an empty barn. It was never es-tablished why they had done it, but they never denied they had. On another occasion, the three brothers had between them killed a cat and had been seen doing so; a different time one of them had cut through the cable of the street lamp just opposite the stationery store. When the lamp duly plummeted down like a stone, it only just missed striking a bicyclist before shattering on the sidewalk. The brothers wrought their destruction with earnest and concentrated expressions, without particularly intending adverse consequences for anyone. When they were asked why they had poured hydrochloric acid over the teacher's car, they said it was because they were curious to see what would happen. That same teacher then bent over backwards to prevent the case from coming before the courts.

Simon, the youngest of the three brothers, had gone to school with the next-door neighbor's son. For a time, the two of them had been friends. Sometimes, Simon came around, and then the boys would play together, or read comics, until the neighbor packed them off outside for the fine weather. The boys never spent any time at Simon's place. The neighbor wasn't sorry. She was unable to picture that apartment over the shop, or imagine anyone living in it, except the invisible invalid.

Ruth's father had died maybe ten years ago. He had driven into the canal by the feed mill. He had been found three weeks later. The car had lain in the canal, with the man inside it, for all of three weeks. No one in the village thought it was an accident.

On Simon, the word was later that he had been on drugs. There were stories that he spent half the year on an island in the Far East somewhere, and one day the paper announced that he had died, and there was something about a long illness, which gave rise to a new surge of rumor. Thomas had moved away, Elias had married and lived at the other end of the village, but in all the years of their being neighbors, the neighbor had never once seen him at Ruth's.

Ruth was the complete opposite of her brothers. She had been terribly gentle as a child, and good at her schoolwork. She was a Girl Scout, she took part in various sports clubs, and was even in charge of one or another of them, and she was active in the Young Church. After school and right up to the time she got married, she helped her father in the shop. But she too was helpless against the darkness of it, and she too disappeared into the back room. When her father died, the family sold the business to a man who already owned a stationery store in the area. The mother stayed in the apartment over the shop. She had a nurse, and Ruth visited her almost every day.

The neighbor had been glad when Ruth moved into the house next door. She hadn't gotten along with the previous people in the house because of some silly business that had happened years ago. On the day they moved in, Ruth and her family had gone around to introduce themselves, and the neighbor had immediately lost her heart to Ruth's two little girls, who were well-behaved but as cheerful and lively as their mother.

Ruth set to work transforming the garden. She took out the bushes that sprouted on the edge of the property, shielding the house from the eyes of strangers, and in their place planted berries. She raised vegetables, and planted the flowerbeds so cleverly that there was always something in bloom. Her husband mowed the lawn—apart from that he was rarely to be seen in the garden. Ruth even set the grill going in the summer months, and carried meat into the house when it was cooked.

Such a nice family, the neighbor had often remarked to her husband, and she had been unable to understand it when one day she learned that the marriage was over and Ruth's husband had moved out. At that, Ruth had for the first time broken down. Ruth, who earlier had endured all the blows of fortune and had never despaired, who had stood by her brothers after their worst misdeeds, and even after the death of her father had walked about the village with a proud and calm expression. It hadn't happened suddenly but gradually, like those slow motion sequences in which the walls of a house break apart and collapse, until there was nothing to be seen but a great cloud of dust. The neighbor had been condemned to watch helplessly as Ruth now stood around in the garden, stooped and with a dull expression, holding her rake in her hand but quite paralyzed.

The neighbor put the card back on the sideboard. She opened the top drawer. There was nothing in it but table linens and napkins. In the second drawer she found some knitting, the beginnings of a pullover, presumably for one of the girls. She shut it, and when she stooped to open the bottom drawer she felt suddenly guilty, and hurriedly shut it again. She straightened up. Next to the birthday cards, there was a crumpled scrap of paper, a list of important items to remember. Carpet slippers, contact lens cleaner, nightgown, reading matter. The neighbor pocketed the piece of paper, possibly in order to throw it away, and then she left the room and left the house, and locked the door after herself.

Even July had been hot that year. Ruth had left the windows open overnight, and when she closed them in the morning it was cool indoors, and it stayed cool until mid-afternoon. But now that there wasn't anyone there to open and shut the windows, the house had heated up from the attic to the basement. The air was stale and dry. Only in the kitchen, where the houseplants stood, was there the humid atmosphere of a hothouse.

It was quiet in the rooms. Sometimes the telephone on the landing rang six, seven, eight times, and once the muffled sound of band music penetrated the house. Someone in the area had turned ninety, and a brass band had turned out to play . The people stood around in the street, children perched on garden fences, grown-ups stood together and chatted in between tunes, and fell silent when the musicians had found their places and began again. They played briskly and without much feeling. They seemed relieved to be able to pack their instruments away. They might at least have put on their uniforms, the neighbor said to her husband, as they walked home.

At night animals found their way into the garden, mostly cats, but also the odd hedgehog, marten, or fox. Once, years before, the neighbor had seen a badger there, rooting in the compost. But no one apart from her had ever seen the badger, and she stopped talking about it when she sensed that no one else believed her.

One evening there was a storm. The tall pine on the other side of the street bent in the wind, and little birch twigs were blown onto the street. The neighbor stood at the window, looking out. One day the pine would surely fall; it was old and sick and should have been cut down a long time ago. But the apartments in the house opposite were short-term rentals, people kept moving in and out, and no one bothered about the garden.

As darkness fell, it started to rain. Rain flurries blew across the street and rattled against the windowpanes. The street lamp swayed in the wind; it seemed to have come to life, as it lunged around wildly in the darkness. The neighbor wondered what she would do if she saw a light on in Ruth's house. Of late, there had been several break-ins. I won't water the garden tomorrow, she thought. She turned on a light, and switched on the TV. By the time she went to bed the wind had eased slightly, but it was still raining.

In the morning the sun was shining, and everything gleamed with wetness. It was cool, the wind had freshened up again, and the clouds blew by in the sky. The neighbor had cycled to the municipal swimming pool. She had swum her lengths, as she did every morning. Now the pool was empty. As she left the baths, the lifeguard locked up after her. The board by the entrance was still marked with the water temperature of the day before.

The neighbor was still on her way home when it started raining again. She cooked lunch. As she ate, she said she wanted to visit Ruth, take her her mail, and perhaps a book. But her husband said she shouldn't get involved. Then she told him about the note she'd found. He didn't know what she was talking about. He looked at her in silence. The neighbor imagined Ruth packing her things, her carpet slippers, her contact lens fluid, her nightgown, and all not knowing when she would come back.

It wasn't until Ruth had asked her to water the flowers that the neighbor learned that it wasn't her first visit to the clinic. There is a beautiful garden there, Ruth said, with big old trees, almost a park. The girls had been picked up that morning by some people (she didn't know them), and just before noon a taxi drew up in front of the house, and Ruth came out with a sports bag, threw a look in the direction of the neighbor's house, where the neighbor was standing behind the lace curtains. She slowly raised her hand, as if in greeting.

The neighbor didn't know why she had pocketed the list, or what it was doing still in her apron pocket. The words *reading matter* had surprised her and moved her, she didn't understand why, after all, it wasn't as though she were related to Ruth or anything.

"But she likes reading so much," she said. Her husband didn't even look up from his plate. She felt tears well up in her eyes, and she quickly stood up and carried the empty dishes into the kitchen.

THROUGH THE NIGHT

It had started to snow in the late afternoon. He was glad he had taken the day off, because the snow was so heavy that within half an hour the streets were white. He saw the super sweep the path up to the door. He was wearing a hood, and on a small dark island, he was fighting a losing battle against the incessantly falling snow.

It was just as well he hadn't gone to the airport to meet her this time. The last time he had bought her some flowers from a vending machine, and talked her into taking the subway all the way into Manhattan. When they had talked on the phone a few days before, she said he shouldn't bother coming to meet her, she would just take a taxi.

He stood by the window and looked out. Even if her flight was on time, the earliest she could be here was in half an hour. But he felt a little restless just the same. He discarded sentences he had prepared and rehearsed over the past weeks. He knew she would demand an explanation, and he knew he didn't have one. He had never had explanations, but he had always been sure of his ground.

An hour later, he was back in front of the window again. It was still snowing, harder than before, it was a real blizzard now. The super had given up the struggle. Everything was white now, even the air seemed to be white, or at least it was the pale gray of encroaching darkness, and that was barely distinguishable from the white of the falling snow. The cars drove slowly and with exaggerated caution. The few pedestrians who were out leaned forward into the wind.

He switched on the TV. All the local stations were full of news of the storm, and it was striking that they had come up with a name for it too, by which they all referred to it right away. In the outer boroughs the chaos was even worse than downtown, and the coast guard reported a flood alert. But the correspondents who had been sent out to cover the breaking news, in bulky down jackets and speaking into microphones with grotesque windshields, were all in high good humor and were tossing snowballs up into the air, and only got serious when they were asked about the scale of the damage and personal injuries.

He called the airline. He was told that on account of the blizzard, the flight had been rerouted to Boston. No sooner had he put the receiver down than the phone rang. She was calling from Boston, saying they might be on their way again at any moment. There were rumors that JFK had been opened again. But there was also a chance they would have to stay the night in Boston. She said she was looking forward to seeing him, and he told her to take care. See you later, she said, and she hung up.

Outside, it was dark now. The snow was falling steadily, falling and falling, and, apart from a few taxis going by at a crawl, there were no more cars about.

He had thought he would be going out for dinner with her, and he felt hungry now. And it would be several hours till she got there. There was nothing in the fridge except a couple of beers, and a bottle of vodka in the freezer with some ice. He thought he should go and buy something to eat. She was bound to be hungry after the long flight. He put on his warm coat, and a pair of rubber boots. They were the only winter shoes he had, and he had hardly worn them. He took an umbrella and went out.

The snow was deep but it wasn't heavy, and it was easy to shuffle through it in his boots. The stores were closed, and in only a few of them had the shop workers taken the trouble to put up a sign to say why they'd gone home early.

He walked across town. Lexington Avenue was covered with snow, and on Park he saw the distant orange blinking lights of the snowplows coming up the avenue in a convoy. Madison and Fifth had already been cleared but they were white again. He had to scale a high snow rampart at the edge of the sidewalk. He sank in, and some snow got in over the top of his boots.

There was someone cross-country skiing in Times Square. The ads were flashing away as normal. Their garish alternation had something ghostly in so much silence. He walked on, up Broadway. Just before he got to Columbus Circle, he saw the lit-up window of a coffee shop. It was a place he had been to before; the manager and the waiters were Greek, and the food was good.

There were only a few customers there. Most of them were sitting at one of the tables in the window that reached down to the ground, drinking beer or coffee, and looking out. The atmosphere was solemn, no one was talking, it was as though they were all witnesses to a miracle.

He sat down at a table, and asked for a beer and a club sandwich. The snow in his boots started to melt. When the waiter brought him his beer, he asked why the place was still open. They hadn't expected there would be this much snow, the waiter said, and now it was too late. Most of them lived in Queens, and it was impossible to get out there as things stood. So they might as well keep the restaurant open.

"Maybe all night," said the waiter, and he laughed.

The way back seemed easier, even though it was still snowing. He had got them to wrap up a sandwich for her, and noticed that he didn't know what she liked. In the end, he asked for ham and cheese. No mayo, no pickles, at least he remembered that.

She had left him a message on the answering machine. There hadn't been any flights out after all, and now Boston was snowed in as well. They were being driven to the station, to catch a train. If everything went according to plan, she would be in Manhattan in four hours. She had left the message an hour ago.

He switched the TV back on. A man was standing in front of a map, explaining how the storm front was moving north along the coast, and had now reached Boston. New York had been through the worst, the man said and smiled, but it would probably go on snowing for the rest of the night.

He switched off the TV and went back over to the window. He wasn't thinking about his sentences any more, he was just looking out at the street. He turned off the main light and switched on the desk lamp. Then he made some tea, sat down on the sofa, and read. At midnight he went to bed.

When the bell rang it was three. Before he could get to the door, it rang again. He pressed the entry button, and held it a moment. Then, though dressed only in shorts and a T-shirt, he stepped out onto the landing and walked toward the elevator. It seemed to take forever.

Of course he knew it was her, but he was strangely surprised when the elevator doors opened and he saw her standing in front of him. She just stood there, her big red suitcase next to her, waiting. He stepped toward her. When he moved to kiss her, she put her arms around him. The elevator doors shut behind him. She said: "I'm just so incredibly tired." He pushed the button, and the doors opened again.

They split the sandwich, and she told him about how the train had stopped in the snow in the middle of nowhere, and had stood there for hours until finally a snowplow had come along and cleared the tracks.

"Of course no one knew what was going on," she said. "I was afraid we'd be there all night. At least I brought some warm clothes with me." He asked if it was still snowing, then looked out into the night himself and saw that it had almost stopped.

"The taxi would only take me to the corner of Lexington," she said. "It couldn't get into your street. I gave the driver twenty dollars and said, please get me to the door, it doesn't matter how. He carried my case all the way. A little Pakistani. Nice man."

She laughed. They had drunk some vodka, and he poured out a refill.

"Well?" she said. "What's this urgent thing you wanted to talk to me about?"

"I love snow," he said.

He stood up and went over to the window. The snow was falling but only in little flakes that drifted down from the sky, sometimes floated up as if they were lighter than air, then subsided again, disappearing against the white sidewalks. "Isn't it beautiful?"

He turned around and looked at her a long time as she sat there sipping her vodka. He said: "I'm glad you've come."

LIKE A CHILD, LIKE AN ANGEL

When the fireworks finished, the few hotel guests who had gathered in front of the hall window clapped. In between the bangs of the rockets, there had been scraps of music, choirs, an organ, and once the pealing of bells. The music came from down by the river, a long way off, and sometimes it was drowned out by the noise of the crowd outside on the streets. At those moments, Eric had the feeling he belonged to this city, these celebrations, these people. The applause on the hotel landing brought him back to himself. Someone closed the window.

A million people had watched the fireworks, said the waiter as he brought breakfast up to the room the next morning. On the way to the airport, Eric calculated: on average, a human being lives to the age of seventy, which is twenty-five thousand days. Therefore, every day one person in twenty-five thousand dies. Of the million people who were watching the fireworks last night, statistically speaking, twenty must already have died.

The taxi drove through a suburb, and Eric saw mothers with children, old people, and a group of girls sitting on a bench waiting for a bus. Suddenly he felt inexplicably moved by something, a feeling that lasted until the taxi drew up in front of the departure lounge. Eric wished the driver a nice day.

Eric worked in the internal accounts department of a multi-national food conglomerate. Roughly two-thirds of his job consisted of visiting the various subsidiaries dotted all over Europe and North America. He had originally taken the job precisely because it involved so much travel. He liked getting around and meeting new people. But over time he had gotten used to it, and the traveling came to seem routine and finally burdensome. It began with his preferring aisle seats on planes, and no longer bothering to unwrap his meals.

He always stayed at classy hotels, he had no real limit on his expenses. By day he worked, and in the evenings colleagues from the various subsidiaries took him out and showed him their cities. They would eat together in expensive restaurants, go to nightclubs, get drunk. Sometimes Eric would take a woman up to his room, not a prostitute, but one of those women you met sitting around the bars of expensive hotels at midnight, looking for something or other. But that wasn't often. Usually, by the time his taxi driver set him down in front of his hotel, Eric was so drunk that, leaving either an absurdly large tip or none at all, he marched straight up to his room.

The hotel rooms were all alike, the restaurants were all

alike, the conversations with colleagues, the airports, the cities. The journeys were always the same, Eric smoked and drank too much, and had headaches in the morning. The worst thing were the times in Eastern Europe. There his companions either ordered vodka, or else the sweet liqueurs they were so proud of, and that, too, were indistinguishable. And on the days after such occasions, the headaches would be worse too.

Valdis, who met Eric at the airport, behaved as though they were old friends, even though they only saw each other a couple of days a year. He should definitely try to stay longer this time, Valdis had said on the phone, when Eric called to announce his latest visit, the city was celebrating its eight hundredth anniversary, and there would be gigantic celebrations.

Valdis was the only man in the local accounts department who could speak German. He used strange expressions, and had a strong accent, and somehow never got to the point. When he went out drinking with Eric, he always insisted on buying for them both. Eric then told him he could put it down on expenses, that way the company would pay. The checks were never for very much, but Eric knew what Valdis made.

Once, Valdis had invited him back to his house. He lived somewhere on the edge of the city in a scuzzy prefab development. The apartment was small and stuffy in its layout and furnishings, and reminded Eric of his parents' place. Then he met Valdis's wife. She was beautiful, and Valdis seemed to be very much in love with her. At any rate, when she was in the kitchen he said he was a very happy man.

After dinner, a bottle of an herb liqueur called balzams was produced (which Eric hated), and then they all moved onto a first name basis. Valdis's wife was called Elza. Eric said it was a beautiful name, and he invited them both to stay whenever they were next in Switzerland. But Valdis said that was hardly likely, such a journey was completely beyond their means. Eric asked if he could do anything else to help.

"No," said Valdis with a smile. "You enjoyed balancing the books, didn't you?"

The rest of the year Eric would never hear anything from Valdis. The greater his astonishment when a letter arrived from him one day, to his home address. When he read the name of the sender on the envelope, he had to stop and think for a moment.

Dear friend, wrote Valdis. Eric was taken aback. Valdis wrote to say something was troubling him. The phrase made Eric laugh. His wife was sick, Valdis wrote, and if Eric remembered the occasion of his previous visit, he would know that even then he had intimated that all was not well. Now it had turned out that Elza had cancer, and could not expect to live more than another two years.

Eric had always liked Valdis, but he couldn't understand what he was doing, writing to him. It struck him as inappropriate and embarrassing. They would see each other in a month anyway. Then Valdis went on to write about his children: the boy was going to high school next year, and his daughter wanted to become an accountant, like her father.

Eric's wife called him for supper. He turned over the thin sheet of letter paper, and read on. There was, he read, one cure for Elza's cancer. A Swiss professor had developed it, a completely new drug that was still undergoing clinical trials. But its results so far on a sample group of patients had been encouraging. In such cases as Elza's a cure was not impossible. At least there was a chance that she might have a few more years to live. Years in which some even more successful therapy might be discovered.

Eric's wife called him again, and he went into the dining room with the letter in his hand. The treatment was expensive, wrote Valdis, quite impossible for someone from his country, for himself, and not cheap even for a Swiss. He had—at this point the writing got smaller, not least because Valdis had reached the bottom of the page— he had never in his life asked anyone for anything. He and his wife had been through some lean times together, without complaining. Nor did they have anything to complain about, really, because they had always been together, and they loved each other. But now he was turning to Eric for help. *You asked me once whether you could do anything for me*, he wrote, *well, now you can do everything*.

Eric put the letter aside, and sat down. His wife asked who the letter was from, and he told her.

"Is that the man with the beautiful wife?"

"She's sick. She's got cancer."

Eric's wife sighed and shrugged her shoulders. Eric didn't tell her of Valdis's appeal to him. He could imagine what she would say.

"They have two kids," he said.

Valdis had told Eric the name of the professor who had pioneered the new form of therapy, and suggested he get in touch with him directly if he had questions. Eric called the professor. He briefly explained the therapy, and talked about the promising results he had obtained with it thus far. He said, yes, he had heard of the case of the wife of Eric's friend. Valdis wasn't really a friend as such, Eric said, it was more that they had professional dealings with one another. Anyway, he was familiar with the case, the professor said again, he had studied in Freiburg with the woman's own specialist. He said the treatment cost something in the order of a hundred thousand francs. And he could not positively guarantee a successful outcome.

"We're talking maybe thirty percent," he said, "at most. I've heard she's an exceptionally beautiful woman."

Thirty percent, thought Eric. Valdis had talked of "encouraging results." To raise a hundred thousand, Eric would have had to sell stock. And it was certain that Valdis would never be in a position to repay him. He hadn't spoken in terms of a loan either. He just wanted the money. Which was understandable, in his position.

Eric sent Valdis an E-mail. He wrote that the best thing would be for them to discuss the matter together, and that they would be seeing each other in two weeks in any case. That was the last he heard, until he called Valdis a week before his departure to phone through his arrival time, and Valdis didn't refer to Elza's illness, just said Eric should try to extend his visit to take in the jubilee celebrations.

Nor did Valdis speak of his wife as they drove from the airport to the company headquarters, and Eric didn't want to be the one to broach the subject either. He praised Valdis's work, and said really he had no reason to come, as everything there was always so shipshape. Valdis said that would be a pity, because where else would Eric get to drink balzams and eat schaschlik.

Eric had reckoned on three days of work. On Saturday he wanted to make a tour of the city, and he had booked his return flight for noon on Sunday. It was not until his arrival that he learned that Friday had been made a holiday, on account of the anniversary celebrations. But if Eric liked, said Valdis, then he would come to the office anyway. Then they would be undistracted, and could work quietly. Eric said they could probably get through it in two days anyway.

"I don't mind," said Valdis. "Then we can talk quietly instead."

Eric had the sense that Valdis was working deliberately slowly. During their lunch break, he stayed sitting down for a long time, and Eric got angry. Valdis didn't mention the situation with his wife, and Eric was certainly not going to bring it up. As in previous years they went out together; Valdis took Eric to an Italian restaurant that had recently opened, and that was supposed to be good. The food was fine but the wine was poor, and overpriced. Valdis knew nothing about wine, but he seemed to take Eric's criticism personally. When they were finished, he made no move to pay the check, as he usually did. Even though Eric wouldn't have allowed it anyway, he still felt annoyed with Valdis, and also because Valdis had persuaded him to drink more of that ghastly balzams, and because he had helped him into his coat after dinner.

Valdis was keen to go to a bar afterwards. "Here are the most beautiful women in the city," he said. Young women who were happy to make the acquaintance of wealthy men from the West. The bar was near the cathedral. The décor was chrome and leather, and the music was so loud that there was no chance of a meaningful conversation. They stood by the bar, Valdis drinking balzams, Eric beer. There were a couple of blond women standing next to them. When Valdis spoke to them, Eric saw how drunk he was. Valdis put his arm round the waist of one of the women, and yelled something in her ear. She seemed not to understand, and raised her eyebrows and gave a puzzled smile. While speaking to the woman, Valdis nodded a couple of times in the direction of Eric. Her face darkened. She shook her head, took her friend by the arm, and pulled her away. Valdis tried to hold the two of them back, grabbed them round the waist, but they twisted out of his hold and disappeared into the crowd. Valdis put his mouth so close to Eric's ear that he could feel his breath.

"Whores," he called out.

Eric paid the check, and left the bar. Valdis came after him. While they walked to the hotel, Valdis said he could get Eric any woman he wanted. It was just a matter of money. Eric thought of Elza. He wondered if Valdis was faithful to her. And what about her? She could certainly have any man she wanted. Valdis staggered and grabbed hold of Eric's arm, before finally pushing his arm through his. A hundred thousand, thought Eric, for a woman. "You're drunk," he said. "I don't want a woman."

Outside the hotel, he put Valdis in a taxi, asked him for the address, and gave the driver some money.

"Kiburgas iela 12," said Valdis. "Third story, left-hand side."

Before Eric closed the taxi door, he asked Valdis if he was okay. Valdis looked at him with moist eyes and said: "You are my friend."

The following morning Eric was in the office early, and had already gotten through several items on the audit before Valdis arrived. Eric said if Valdis felt up to it, they might be able to finish the job today. Valdis seemed pretty monosyllabic, but he worked quickly and didn't complain. He was pale and took a lot of bathroom breaks, and to judge by his face he probably had a headache. At

lunchtime they sent out for sandwiches, and by late afternoon they had finished the audit.

Valdis asked what plans Eric had for the evening. Valdis
looked as though he'd do better to go home, said Eric. He
was pretty tired himself and would just have a snack at
the hotel, and maybe go to the movies. Valdis nodded and
asked whether they would see each other the next day. Eric
said he would call him.

"I must show you the city," said Valdis. "And the celebrations. Eight hundred years is a long time."

Valdis called while Eric was at breakfast. The woman
at reception gave him a note with the number on it, and
said the gentleman had asked to be called back. Eric went
out on the street, and wandered through the Old Town,
which he had seen only at night thus far. At about noon,
he returned to the hotel and called Valdis. It was Elza who
picked up. She said her husband had been waiting for Eric
to call, but half an hour ago he had taken the children into
town. He had said he wanted to see something of the celebrations. The symphony orchestra was playing in the cathedral square.

"That's where I've just come from," said Eric.

Elza said Valdis had said he would go by the hotel to
see if Eric was there. Did she not feel like coming out at
all, Eric asked. No, said Elza, she didn't like crowds.

"I'm just enjoying having the place to myself. It happens
rarely enough."

"What about the fireworks later on?"

"I'm not sure."

Eric said he might call later on. Then he asked Elza how she was feeling.

"Fine, thank you," she said. "I'm sorry we won't see each other this time. Yesterday I felt sure you would come over."

"Valdis didn't say anything."

"He said you wanted to go to the movies."

"I think we were both pretty tired. We're not getting any younger, after all."

Elza laughed. She said she had rarely seen Valdis as drunk as he was that night. The taxi driver had brought him to the front door, to be sure he made it safely up the steps.

"I gave the man a big tip," said Eric.

Elza sounded fine, and after Eric hung up he wondered for a moment whether she might not actually be sick at all. But then he thought, no, she's just brave. Presumably she didn't know that Valdis had come to him for money.

Eric went downstairs and asked the receptionist for the way to the market. Valdis had said that was something he absolutely had to see. He would be back in the evening, said Eric, in case anyone called for him.

The market was housed in four former zeppelin hangars behind the railway station. There were some old women standing on the pavement outside, selling plastic bags that had the names of various western products on them. Everyone here seemed to have something they were trying to sell.

Some people sat on the ground, with just an old cardboard box in front of them on which they'd laid out a few things, tapes, ballpoints, broken toys.

Eric didn't stay long at the market. He found it all pretty dismal. He went back to the Old City. There were flags up in the streets. That morning already there had been choral singing on the stages that had been put up everywhere. More and more people were squeezing into the narrow alleyways, holding hands and walking quickly, as though they had somewhere to get to.

Eric walked back to his hotel. The woman at reception told him a man had come asking for him. He had waited for at least an hour, and then he had gone away again. He had said he would try again later. Eric asked her to change his return flight from Sunday to Saturday. Then he took one of the taxis that were lined up outside the hotel, and gave the driver Valdis's address, Kiburgas iela 12.

He had the taxi stop at the edge of the project, got out and walked about among the crumbling tenement blocks. They were widely separate, with lawns in between them, and the occasional birch tree. The grass hadn't been cut for a long time, and it sprouted up between the pavement slabs and in the cracks of the curbs.

Eric looked for the house that Valdis and Elza lived in. Suddenly he couldn't remember their surname. There were only numbers next to the buttons at the entrance. He tried the door. It was unlocked. He climbed up the steps. In some places, the wallpaper was in shreds.

The individual apartment doors also only had numbers. On the third floor, Eric stopped and listened. He thought he could hear a vacuum cleaner, but he wasn't sure which apartment the sound was coming from. He stood there for two or three minutes, thinking about Elza, and hoping she might just come and open the door. Then he wondered what he would say if she did. Finally, he went back down the steps, as quietly as he had gone up them.

He walked through the project. There was no one around, except for a few kids playing. The road ended in a large cul-de-sac, in the middle of which there was a flat garage building. A man was leaning over the engine of a car. He scratched his head. Then he looked up. Eric gave him a nod, but the man only looked suspiciously at him as he moved on.

Eric crossed the patch of grass between the last two blocks. At the very edge of the terrain there were a couple of vegetable patches, then an overgrown piece of wasteground, and then forest. Eric followed a narrow path that led into the forest, and then immediately lost itself among the trees. The air was damp, and Eric began to sweat. It was very quiet. He wondered what he was doing there.

When he got back to the hotel at about eight, the woman at reception handed him an envelope with his name on it. Valdis wrote that he had been told Eric would be leaving tomorrow. So they probably would not be able to meet after all. He would be watching the fireworks this evening, at the apartment of friends. If Eric needed anything, he could find him there, or at home tomorrow morning. And if he didn't hear anything more from Eric, then he merely wished him a safe flight back, and all the best in the future. He looked forward to seeing him next year.

The air in Eric's room was warm and close. All at once, he felt very tired. He opened the window and lay down.

He was awakened by the fireworks. He stepped up to the window, but he couldn't see anything from there. He went out into the hall. Some hotel guests stood in front of the window next to the elevator. Bengal lights were reflected on their faces. Three times three hundred and thirty meters made a kilometer, said an elderly man. In the shadow, next to the stairs, stood the young woman from the hotel bar, watching the spectacle over the heads of the guests. When the fireworks were over, she hurried down the steps, back to work. A group of Americans applauded halfheartedly. It was worth it after all, a woman said in German. She had already been asleep, and merely thrown a coat over her nightdress. But it had been worth it. Eric wondered what it was all for. With the money they had gone through here, it would have been possible to pay for Elza's course of treatment, three times over.

The other hotel guests wandered back to their rooms. Eric looked at his watch. It was a little before midnight, too late to call Valdis's friends. He went downstairs to the bar.

"We're closed now," said the bar woman.

"Just one little beer?" Eric asked beseechingly.

The woman smiled, shrugged her shoulders, and raised her eyebrows in apology. Eric sat down on a barstool, and watched her as she counted up the till. He put a banknote down, enough to pay for the beer many times over. He asked the woman what her name was. She looked at him reproachfully. Then she took a beer bottle out of the refrigerator tray, opened it, and set it down in front of Eric. She pushed the banknote away.

"I've already done the accounts," she said, picked up the bag containing the money, and crossed the lobby to the reception. She wore tight black pants in some shiny stuff. Eric followed her with his eyes. She walked with a light, quick step, almost a hop, and Eric remembered how she had run down the stairs when the fireworks were over. She had taken them two at a time. It looked almost as if she were flying, like a child, like an angel. At the turn in the stairs, she had put one hand on the balustrade, swung round, and disappeared.

FADO

Everything in Lisbon was damp. Even though it wasn't raining, the streets were dark with moisture. Moss sprouted from the walls and facades, and the sky was full of clouds.

I had wanted to take ship and go, but there was a delay in the loading of the freighter and I was forced to wait. I had already moved my things into my cabin. Lisbon had nothing for me. In my mind, I had already said goodbye to Europe, I thought what lay ahead would be more interesting than what lay behind. But the prospect of waiting on the ship was deadly. There's nothing more boring than a ship in port.

I walked into the city. I spent the whole day tramping the streets without looking at anything. I strolled through obscure parts of town, where men had spread porn mags on big cloths and were selling them. I sat in cafes, watching the people getting off ferries and going to work. From up on the hill I stared down at the city, and out to sea, till it lost itself in haze. Toward evening I got back to the port, and heard that now the ship wasn't going till the next day, which was a Sunday. I headed into the city again, to get something to eat. In a side street I found a restaurant where they played fado music.

The food was poor but I liked the music, it suited my mood. I sat on after my meal was finished. I had already drunk half a liter of wine, and I ordered another. The other half, I said to the waiter, a little dark-skinned man, but he didn't react. I felt better, and started to jot a few things down. I had just noted some foolish thought when a young woman came up to my table and asked me, in English, whether I wanted to come and sit with her and her friend. I had noticed her earlier. She was sitting with another woman at a table near me. While they ate, they both laughed a lot, and looked across at me a couple of times.

"You looked so all alone," she said. "We're Canadian."

I took her invitation and followed her with my glass and carafe of wine.

"I'm Rachel, and this is Antonia," she said.

We sat down.

"I'm Walter."

"Like Walt Whitman," said Antonia. "Do you keep a diary?"

"Oh, I write whatever comes into my head," I said. "It's almost as good as talking."

"My father always used to say only intelligent people can bear solitude," said Antonia.

"Being alone doesn't make anyone intelligent," I said.

It was past eleven. The fado singer packed up his guitar, and came over to our table. He seemed to know Rachel and Antonia. He sat down, and we talked about Lisbon and fado music.

"The last piece was nice," said Antonia, "what was it called?"

"If you don't know where you're going, why don't you stop walking," the fado singer quoted. "Heart of mine, I won't go with you anymore."

"Amalia," he said, and his face suddenly looked ridiculously tormented. "*This strange sort of life.*"

"What sorts of life are there?" Antonia asked.

"Long, for one," said Rachel, "or short. Whichever."

"My heart lives on wasted lives," the fado singer continued to quote.

Rachel asked me what sort of life mine was.

I said I didn't know. Presumably none at all. With both her hands, she outlined the shape of a woman in the air.

"Woman . . ." said the fado singer, and then some nonsense or other. I knew what he was after, and I knew he wasn't going to get it tonight. He seemed to know it too. But just the same, he wrote down his phone number on a napkin, and passed it to Rachel. He said they could call him anytime. Any time at all. Then he shook hands all around, and went.

"Man . . ." said Rachel, and laughed. Antonia told her to stop being stupid.

"Would you have gone with him, then?" asked Rachel, drawing up her eyebrows in surprise. "Do you fancy bullfighters?"

"Portugal doesn't have any bullfighters," said Antonia. "He had a nice voice."

Rachel laughed. She had met a man once with a nice voice. "I only knew him from talking on the phone. And when I finally got to see him . . . he was indescribable."

Antonia said Rachel should stop being stupid again. Rachel said the pitch of a man's voice was important. Men with low voices had a lot of testosterone. My voice, for instance, was deep.

Rachel laughed and said they had fixed with Luis to meet up in the disco. "The little waiter, you know. Once he's finished here."

For the past three weeks, Rachel and Antonia had been touring around Europe. In a week they would be flying home, from Barcelona. Rachel talked about the small town in Canada where they both came from, and Antonia kept interrupting and correcting things she was saying. I listened and didn't say a lot. I was just glad to have some company.

The last of the customers left, and Luis put the chairs on the table and swept the floor. Then he walked over to our table.

"This is a friend," said Rachel. "He's coming to the disco with us."

Luis said it wasn't far. His English wasn't up to much, and he had a heavy accent.

"What a low voice," said Rachel, and she laughed. She asked Luis if he had a lot of testosterone. He asked what that was.

"Toro," said Rachel. "You like a bull?"

Antonia told Rachel to stop it. She was drunk.

"You bull, me cow," said Rachel. Luis looked at her in bafflement.

"You Tarzan, me Jane," said Rachel.

"Tarzan." Luis nodded. "We go."

Luis said he would show us the best disco in Lisbon. He walked very fast, so that we had trouble keeping up. We zigged and zagged down narrow little streets. After just a few, I had no idea of my bearings. Rachel was talking about her boyfriend, who was a pilot in the air force.

"He's got a really low voice," she said, "like a prop plane."

I asked Antonia whether she too had a boyfriend. She shook her head. She had just started university in Montreal, and didn't know anyone there.

"She had a boyfriend but she broke his heart," said Rachel.

"Nonsense," said Antonia, "he was never my boy-friend."

"Hey, Luis," said Rachel, "*slow down!*"

After half an hour, we were finally there. The place we were standing outside was scuzzy and small. Luis knew the doorman, but we still had to pay a ridiculously large sum of money to get in.

It was dark in the disco, except on the slightly raised dance floor, which was brightly lit. It was empty, but some of the tables had people at them. It was almost completely guys. The music was loud. We sat down at the bar, drank, and talked. Luis didn't say much. Suddenly he stood up, climbed up onto the dance floor, turned his back to us, and started dancing in front of a large wall-mirror. I could see his face reflected in it, he was looking serious and concentrated. I thought he was staring into his own eyes. His movements were mechanical and aggressive. I asked Rachel to dance. Antonia remained behind at the bar, alone.

I had been feeling fairly drunk, but the long walk had sobered me up. I danced with Rachel for a long time. We looked at each other, Luis seemed only to have eyes for himself, in the mirror. After a half hour or so, he said there was nothing happening, he knew some better places. Antonia said she wanted to go to bed. Rachel whispered something in her ear. She said she wanted to go to bed too. She laughed.

The four of us walked down empty streets. Rachel had taken my arm. Luis tried to take her other arm, but she shook him off. She said she wasn't a baby. Luis instead linked arms with Antonia, who didn't resist, and walked along stiffly beside him, not looking at him. Luis said he came from Faro, in the south of Portugal, but there was no work there. Then he was silent. None of us spoke. We walked more slowly than we had on the way there, more carefully, as though to postpone the goodnights. Too little had happened, and then again too much for an easy leave-taking.

Rachel and Antonia shared a room in a private house. When we got to the house, they said goodnight, and we kissed on the cheek. Antonia unlocked the door, and went inside. Rachel stood in the open doorway for a brief moment, with a childlike smile. Then Luis went up to her, and forced her back to the staircase. I followed them. The door fell shut behind me with a crash. Then there was silence.

The staircase was dimly lit by a single bulb. Antonia was waiting on the staircase, looking down to us. Rachel and Luis stood facing each other, and staring.

"Goodnight," said Rachel.

"I'm coming up," said Luis.

"We're tired. Thanks for the fun evening."

Rachel followed Antonia up the stairs. Luis and I came after the two women.

"Goodnight," Rachel said again.

"I'm not tired," said Luis.

"But we are."

"Come on, let's go," I said to Luis, and took him by the arm.

"I call the police," said Luis. "I tell them everything."

"Call the police. Do you think they'll believe you?" said Rachel mockingly. She turned to Antonia. "Go on!"

Antonia pressed the bell, and a shrill metallic ringing came from inside the apartment. Luis climbed up another step. I passed him, and drew myself up in front of him. I pressed him back against the wall, but I knew right away that he was stronger than me, and that my chances of being able to hold him back were nil. His body was tensed, but he didn't move. I was surprised he didn't put up any struggle. Antonia rang the bell a second time. We stood there in silence, then finally the door opened. A fifty-year-old woman in a dressing gown peered out. She didn't say anything. I let go of Luis.

"I call the police now," he said once more, and went down the stairs.

"Get lost!" Rachel called after him. "You fucking idiot!"

"Come on in," Antonia said to me, and the three of us stepped into the apartment, and went into their room. All this time, the landlady hadn't said a word. She looked very tired, and she disappeared.

"Are you allowed gentlemen callers here?" I asked.

"I hope you're no gentleman," said Rachel. "Do you want a beer?"

She took three bottles out of the wardrobe and opened them. The beer was tepid. We felt a little easier, and at the same time more excited. We all talked at once, and laughed a lot.

"What an asshole," said Rachel.

"He took us to dinner," said Antonia. "Maybe he thought . . ."

"They won't come," said Rachel. "The police. And so what if they do. We'll just throw the stuff out the window."

She asked me if I wanted any. She had sat down on the bed beside Antonia. I shook my head.

Rachel said they were almost out of money. Could I lend them some? I gave them the last of my escudos. It wasn't much, and I wouldn't be needing it anyway, on the ship. Rachel whispered something to Antonia. Antonia pulled a face. She said she was going to take a shower, and she went out into the hallway.

"What was that you whispered?" I asked.

"I asked her what we would do for you in return for fifty thousand escudos."

She laughed, and sprawled back on the bed.

"What we need now is a really wide bed," she said. Antonia came back, and Rachel went to the shower. She stopped in the doorway and told us to behave ourselves. "Remember, Mama'll be back in a moment."

When I left the two of them, it was just starting to get light. We embraced. Rachel handed me an empty beer bottle.

"In case he's waiting outside," she said. "That way you can defend yourself."

I went out on the street. There was no one around. I walked through the empty city with my beer bottle in my hand. I felt stupid. After a couple of hundred yards, I dropped it in the garbage. I hesitated for a moment, and then I threw away the piece of paper where Rachel and Antonia had written down their addresses for me.

Once I was on the ship, I lay down, but I wasn't able to sleep, and soon stood up again. I trotted through the city some more. When I was tired, I went into a little church where Mass was just being said. I sat down in the back pew, and listened. From time to time, I managed to make out the odd word. At the end, the worshipers turned to both sides and shook hands with their neighbors. I had no one sitting next to me. I hurried to be first out of the church.

ALL THAT'S MISSING

The secretary collected David from the airport. She had come in her own car. She asked if it was okay with him if she took the A4. He said he didn't mind either way, he didn't know the first thing about the place. After that they were silent, until the skyscrapers of the Docklands area came into view.

"Over recent years, the docklands have turned into London's most important financial and business center," said the secretary. "Living space is of the highest quality. There are also abundant facilities for rest and recreation."

She talked like a tour guide, it sounded like something she had rattled off many times before. It was an area of twenty-two square kilometers, she said, larger than the City of London and the West End put together. David would find delightful pubs down on the river, there were fine shops, cinemas, and even an indoor stadium seating twelve thousand people. She talked about swing-bridges, sailing ships, and a city farm with real animals. She said her name was Rosemary.

"The Isle of Dogs is at the heart of the Docklands area," she said. "The name is presumably given on account of the royal dog kennels which used to be located here. But my friends say the name might as well come from the many financial institutions that have their offices here."

Rosemary laughed apologetically. She said most of her friends worked in other trades. She asked David what his hobbies were. *Hobbies?* he asked, and looked at her in puzzlement. What he was interested in, then? He said he wasn't interested. *I am not interested*, he said. *In what?* asked Rosemary. *In general*, he said.

David didn't know how long he was going to stay. The initial arrangement was for six months. A tour of duty, they had called it in Switzerland, a mission was how his new boss referred to it. The London branch had experienced difficulties recruiting qualified staff, and they had come to David because he was single. When he hesitated, he was informed that his taking the offer wouldn't harm his advancement prospects, quite the contrary. A certain geographical flexibility was expected with the job.

It was a Friday, and the boss introduced David to his future colleagues, before telling him to come back on Monday. For now, he was just to find his feet in London, get moved into his apartment, and take a look around the area. Greenwich, the place where time began, was just across the river. He wished him a pleasant weekend.

"Rosemary will take you to your new home," said the boss.

Rosemary was, again, taciturn. She drove south along the Thames, through building sites. It wasn't far. They passed a small park, and Rosemary pointed out the building complex behind it, a line of interconnected brick towers. Some of the brick towers were on the river, others faced the park.

"Here it is," she said, and turned off the main road. She waved to the security guard who manned the gate, and he waved back to her. She parked the car in one of the visitors' spots in the underground parking lot, and said she would take David up to his apartment. He said that wouldn't be necessary, he had hardly anything in the way of luggage, but she insisted.

"I'll show you everything," she said.

The apartment belonged to the company. It was on the seventh floor, facing north to the park. From the balcony, there was a view of Canary Wharf and the Thames.

"That's where we've come from," said Rosemary, pointing to the high-rise blocks. She had followed David out onto the balcony.

The last person to have lived here was a Swede, she said, but everything had been cleaned and disinfected since. The Swede had been transferred to New York, he was still very young, and had outstanding career prospects.

"It's getting cool," she said. "Shall we go back inside?"

She took David through the apartment, showed him the walk-in closet in the bedroom, the Italian designer kitchen, the vast TV set on wheels in the living room. She was familiar with the apartment, having picked up the Swede from the airport two years ago now, and taken him here. Perhaps she's been here since as well, thought David. Her eyes had shone when she was speaking about the Swede.

Rosemary was a great fan of the apartment. Twice she said she lived in a tiny little terraced house in Stepney, which was quite handy, but it was so much nicer to live here, among other financial sector workers, and just a short walk to work.

She said there was another TV outlet in the bedroom. If he was ever ill, it was an easy matter to roll the TV across. Magnus, the Swede, had often been ill. She shrugged her shoulders. It was odd that he looked so fit and healthy, and was always so cheerful. He had some kind of health problem.

Then all at once Rosemary was in a hurry. She wished David a pleasant weekend, and left. He looked at his watch. It was five o'clock.

Once he was all alone, he went to the bathroom and washed his hands. He looked at his new premises again. The rooms were clean and bright, the furnishings tasteful. On the coffee table in the sitting room, there was a brochure for the development. The name of the complex was *The Icon*. Strange and inappropriate name for it, thought David. He thought of the icons in the windows of an auction house that he had often passed, those rigid and attentive women's faces that all looked alike and gazed at him in astonishment through the bullet-proof glass.

David sat down on the sofa, and started leafing through the brochure. The towers comprised a hundred and fifty units on eleven stories. An appendix at the back showed the floor plans for the various types of unit. David's was one of the smaller ones, it was type G. On either side of him were three-room apartments that were type H.

David went out onto the balcony, with the brochure in his hand. Dark clouds with white edges passed across the sky. A stormy wind was blowing. It had grown distinctly cold. When David turned to go back inside, he saw a Japanese woman standing on the balcony next to his. She was standing there quite still, looking at him. She was no more than five yards away. He quickly turned and went in.

He stood in his living room and thought: I should have introduced myself. The Japanese woman was his new neighbor, they were bound to run into each other in the hallway, or on their balconies, or in the gym. For a moment, he toyed with the idea of ringing her bell and introducing himself. But he didn't know whether people did that here or not. The simplest thing would have been to say hello to her when he saw her on her balcony. Spontaneous and uncomplicated. But if he went out there again, it would look as though he had gone out to engineer some kind of conversation.

Still holding the brochure, David walked through the apartment. He went over the list of specifications. Everything was there. The Hansgrohe bath taps were a little disappointing, but he liked the doors of solid maple, which fell shut with a satisfying thunk. In the living room he got down on his knees to examine the quality of the carpeting. He remembered kneeling in church, as a child. The feeling of one's own insignificance, and forgiveness. That had been a kind of happiness. Not to have to make any decisions, not to have any responsibility. Sometimes he wished he could have that state back again. In his memory, it was always springtime. The shadows were cool and hard-edged. His mother took him by the hand.

David's knees began to ache, and he stood up and carried a chair out onto the balcony, and sat in it. No sign of the Japanese woman. He shivered.

Tourist boats were going up and down the Thames. The park was almost empty. At the far end of it was a children's playground. Three children were sitting on swings; from time to time he could hear a random scream. David heard the tinkling of a mechanical piano. *Greensleeves*, he hummed along to it. All at once, the tune broke off. The children didn't react, and carried on on their swings.

On the meadow was a brightly colored kite, the size of a man. At first, David supposed it was a man, then he saw someone with light, thinning hair backing away from it quite quickly, and then the kite lifted into the air, climbed up, and finally hung there, wobbling slightly. The man's hair was the same color as his face. He had a backpack and a pair of sunglasses. At the sight of him, David was filled with a vague sense of the sadness of life.

The balconies were now in shadow. There was no one on any of them, though a few had garden furniture of cheap white plastic. David thought of a deckchair he had once seen, made out of oiled robinia wood. It was a construction of striking simplicity, two arc forms pushed together so that one made the seat, the other the back rest. He came close to buying it, even though his apartment in Switzerland didn't have a balcony. The deckchair folded away to next to nothing, the salesman had said. Now David had a balcony. But it was autumn already, and he couldn't see himself with the leisure to be outside during the coming months.

He was to feel at home here, the boss had said to him—it sounded like an order. David wasn't looking forward to the months, the year ahead. My God, he thought, this isn't where I want to be.

He wasn't hungry, but he ate the sandwiches he had made himself at home. He wasn't sure whether they served meals on the short flight to London, and so he had packed something to eat. Once, flying to Milan, there hadn't been anything to eat, and he had felt sick, and it had spoiled the entire day. But on the flight to London, there had been an in-flight snack, a sandwich and pasta salad and a bar of chocolate with the coffee. Meals on planes had always fascinated and disgusted David in equal measure. Even the question, beef or chicken. And then the meal itself, which seemed to have little to do with either—some unspecified meat in nasty plastic dishes. The plane had flown through any weather, and was now up in the blue beyond the clouds. That was how David imagined Paradise, readymade meals under a blue sky, that was how he pictured Hell.

David sat hunched on the sofa in his living room. When he went to throw away the wrapping of his sandwiches, he noticed he didn't have any garbage bags. He tore a page out of his notebook and wrote down: "garbage bags." He would make up a list of all that was missing. And tomorrow he would go shopping.

Happiness is a question of attitude, he thought. London was a wonderful city, so everyone always said. He would go out to concerts, to films, to musicals. He would meet people. He had already begun to strike up a relationship with Rosemary. He would call her tomorrow. And maybe he would get to meet the Japanese woman in the next-door apartment. It occurred to him that she might not live alone. The thought cast him down.

He went into the kitchen, to make himself some tea. He opened all the cupboards. Then he wrote down on his shopping list: teabags. And followed that with: coffee, coffee filters, sugar, cream. And then: food.

Tomorrow he would visit Greenwich, which was what his boss had recommended.

When David woke up the next morning, it was already past ten o'clock. He was trying to bang on the alarm clock until he realized that the ringing was coming from the telephone. It was Rosemary. She asked if he had started to get acclimatized yet. She hadn't woken him, she hoped. He had been out on the balcony, said David, and hadn't heard the ringing.

Rosemary said she could come over if he liked, and show him the area. Shops and restaurants. David thanked her. He was sure he could manage. It really wasn't any trouble, Rosemary said. She wasn't doing anything. She hated weekends.

"I was going to go to Greenwich," said David.

"Lovely," said Rosemary, "the meridian. You can stand astride the line, with your legs in different hemispheres."

The best thing to do was to take the light railway to the southernmost tip of the peninsula, and from there take the Foot Tunnel under the Thames. If he liked, she could show him. He said, thank you, that was fine.

The sky was overcast, but it hadn't begun raining yet. The light railway was unmanned. At first, David didn't notice, then he was a little disquieted by it. The trains went past each other, apparently undirected, remote-controlled from some hub God knows where.

Without picking it up, David scanned a story in the newspaper that had been left in the seat opposite. A child's body had been found near Tower Bridge. A colored boy of five or six was drifting in the river. A passerby had spotted the body. The child had had his arms and legs cut off. The man who had found it was receiving psychological counseling.

There was a little park at the end of the Isle of Dogs. David stared across the Thames at the white buildings on the other side of the river. They looked powerful and silent, as if out of some other time, some better time. At the top of the hill stood the observatory, where, as David had read in his guide, a red ball was lowered every day at twelve o'clock. Once, ships had set their clocks by this ball. Today the only reason it was lowered was because it had always been lowered.

Tower Bridge was upstream. When David saw the muddy water of the Thames sliding past, he had to think of the dead boy. The notion of having to walk under the river was suddenly intolerable to him.

David went shopping. Everything was incredibly expensive.

He stacked the things in his empty kitchen cupboards and refrigerator. It was soothing to see so much food. This can keep me going for at least two weeks, he thought to himself. He might get through one or another thing, like the milk, but at least he wouldn't starve. And then, when his supplies were used up, he could go on for probably another month. He tried to remember for how long hunger-strikers stayed alive, when the newspapers wrote about such people. Was it seven weeks? Eight?

In the afternoon he went back to the supermarket, and bought more food. This time, he had an eye on long life. He bought powdered milk and canned vegetables, chocolate, and deep-frozen ready meals.

On Sunday, David called his father. His father didn't ask him any questions. He talked about the neighbor's cat, which had been run over by a truck. He had found it outside his garden gate, it had been completely flat, rolled out, there was hardly any blood on it. The misfortune seemed to amuse his father.

"Here, they found the body of a kid drifting in the river," said David, "it had no arms and no legs."

He was still talking when he switched on the TV. He flicked through the channels till he found a program that showed a Japanese man passing his hand three or four inches above the naked body of a Japanese woman. The woman seemed to be becoming aroused by it, even though her eyes were shut and she couldn't see what was going on. David said goodbye to his father, and turned up the sound. The Japanese man was talking about the transference of sexual energy. The whole thing was some pseudo-scientific investigation; obviously, the only thing that mattered was showing images of naked women.

The ostensible scientist had something else up his sleeve. This time he set another naked woman, Japanese again, in front of a television screen that was showing images of a Japanese couple copulating. This second woman was wearing headphones. She showed clear signs of sexual excitement. The original Japanese woman was still lying on the bed next door, and she was very excited too, even though nothing was being done to her, or perceivable to her. The scientist explained that the sexual energy transferred itself from the first woman to the second. How and by what means this transference occurred he did not explain.

The two Japanese women had the generic ugliness of European or American performers in porn films that David had seen from time to time. That is, they didn't have ugly faces, or ugly bodies. It seemed rather to be some kind of inner ugliness, lubricity or squalor. He remembered one film, in which naked women had been wrapped in cling wrap. He switched off the TV. Cling wrap, he put down on his shopping list.

He thought of the Japanese woman next door to him, tried to fix his concentration on her. His hand moved back and forth over her naked body. He liked the idea that his neighbor was lying on her own bed in her own flat, feeling some energy reaching her from somewhere, exciting her in some irresistible way. But he wondered whether his own state of excitement had any influence on the Japanese woman.

Then he thought about the dead kid that had been found. He was curious to learn more about the case. That seemed to him the priority just then. He left his apartment. He spent a long time looking for a newsstand. The newspaper, when he finally found one, didn't have much more information than he already knew.

The police had christened the little boy Adam, and there was talk about a violent end. The boy was wearing orange shorts, and it was thought he had been in the water for about ten days. There were strangulation marks on his neck. A police inspector told the newspaper he had never come across a similar case, and he vowed to keep on at the case until the riddle was solved.

The riddle consisted of seven half-burned-down candles that had been found on the banks of the Thames. They were wrapped in a white cloth that had a name on it. The name was Adekoye Jo Fola Adeoye, and it was thought to be fairly common in Nigeria, he read.

David considered going to Tower Bridge, but then he changed his mind. He was unable to picture the dead boy. Each time he tried, he couldn't do any better than those pictures that were screened to elicit contributions to famine charities.

He wondered if anyone would look for him if he failed to show up to work on Monday. Presumably Rosemary would be sent. She didn't have a key to the apartment, as she stressed. If he didn't open the door and let her in, she would have to go away, and try again the next day. The police wouldn't be alerted until three or four days had passed. First they would ring, then the super would unlock the door. The police were the first to step inside, followed by the super and Rosemary. She screamed, a short, stifled scream, and then threw herself round the super's neck. It was like in the movies. The policemen would make long, serious faces. David's body would be lying on the bed, arms and legs severed, the sheets soaked with blood. His trunk would be buried in a normal-sized coffin, even though a child's coffin would have done.

David sat in his living room. He was full of a wild rage, a rage against the people who had killed and mutilated the innocent boy. He wanted to do something, to bring about some change. But the people who understood the world didn't do anything to change it. And the people who changed the world, didn't understand it. David wasn't sure whether he himself understood anything or not. He was just sure he wouldn't ever change anything. He could picture himself dropping the TV set off the balcony into the park, or taking an ax to the Hansgrohe fittings in the bathroom. With a single blow, he shattered the washbasin. Water spurted from the pipes. He ripped down the shower curtains, he attacked the mirror with his ax, and it shattered into a thousand pieces. He swept the crockery out of the kitchen cupboards, and knocked over the refrigerator. The TV exploded at the foot of the building. Blood splashed down onto the carpet.

David dropped to his knees. He ran his fingers through the carpet tassels. He lay on the carpet, writhing like a sick animal. He thought of the dead cat, the mutilated boy, the Japanese women and the pseudoscientist, and the man with the kite. He thought about building a kite with his father as a boy. He saw his father's expression, the concentration and the careful movements with which he assembled the pieces of wood and draped the colorful silk paper over them, fixed the string to the cross. When they flew the kite, David felt as though it was he himself who was speeding up into the air, steered but barely held by the frail string his father held in his hands.

David thought about how someone somewhere in this city had severed Adam's limbs, his little arms and legs, with an ax, a carpet cutter, he couldn't imagine. Someone would have to atone for what had been done to Adam.

David saw himself building a kite for the little boy. He wasn't able to tell him much more than how to glue the wooden struts together, how to fix the string to them, the type of glue you used to attach the paper. He saw the child holding the kite, he saw himself running across a large meadow, with the string in his hand, both of them now were running. Let go, shouted David, and Adam let go of the kite, and it shot up into the air. David saw himself standing in a meadow, with the string in his hand. He looked up, Adam looked up. He felt the gentle tug of the kite. He was exhausted from running. Then Adam went over to him, and he handed him the string and laid his hands on his shoulders and said, careful, very slowly, I'll hold you. It was just a kite, but Adam would remember it, even if the world split into two halves.

It was very quiet in the apartment. Only now did David register the quiet noises coming from the apartments on either side. He heard running water, footfalls, a radio. He got up, and went out onto the balcony. There was the Japanese woman, watering her plants that were growing in large ceramic pots. He said hello, and she said hello back.

"I'm your new neighbor," he said.

"*Nice to meet you*," said the Japanese woman, with a smile.

"*Nice to meet you, too*," said David. He wanted to say something else, but instead he went back into his apartment. There's no hurry, he thought, everything will sort itself out.

THE STOP

We sat on our packs on the platform. Daniel and I had taken off our T-shirts and were sitting there stripped to the waist, Marianne was wearing cut-off jeans and a bikini top. We were sweating. The tin roof cracked in the heat, and the hot air simmered over the rails. The train would be at least two hours late, the stationmaster had told us. For once, we weren't even annoyed; it struck us as miraculous that there should be trains running in this heat.

"Too bad we don't have any music," said Marianne.

The station café was shut. Daniel said he would go into the village and find some ice cream. He was gone a long time, and when he finally came back the ice cream was already all soft, and we ate it in big bites. Then we heard the whistle of a locomotive. Not even one hour had passed. In the harsh light, a train emerged. It looked as though it were hovering over the rails. Very slowly it came nearer. The stationmaster came out of his office. He was wearing a short-sleeved shirt and a cap. Slowly the train drew into the station, and moved past us. The brakes squealed long and loud. The cars were old. They were painted white, and had red crosses painted on the sides. At last the squealing stopped, and the train jerked to a halt. Then there was silence.

The white train stood there, and nothing happened. Only the telephone kept ringing in the station office, and finally the stationmaster went back into his office, and shortly afterwards the telephone stopped ringing. A fat man in black clothes rapidly crossed the parking lot next to the station. He was sweating, and mopped his brow with a white handkerchief. Shortly before he reached the train, a door opened, the man went inside, and the door shut again.

"Your back is getting all red," said Marianne. "Do you want me to put some lotion on you?"

"What is it with that train?" asked Daniel. He got up and walked down the platform to the very end of the train.

"All sick people," he said as he came back. "A special train, going to Lourdes."

I noticed that the blind in one of the windows had been pushed very slightly up. A face appeared in the narrow crack. Someone was looking at us. Then blinds started going up in some of the other windows, and other faces peered out at us. Some people dangled their arms out of the windows. In some compartments there was no one looking, but even there the blinds had been pushed up a little, and I could see beds with people lying on them, moving. I saw a back, a head, a leg, sometimes a pillow that was being turned over. The sick people seemed to be in constant movement, they really seemed not to be well, they must be in pain, or suffering from the heat. They seemed to me to be very far away from us. A nun in white robes and a white winged bonnet was looking at us from one window. Her face bore a vaguely triumphant expression.

"All sick people," said Marianne. "Honestly, you'd have thought they'd never seen a bikini in their lives, the way they're staring." She stopped rubbing sunscreen into me, turned away from the train, and pulled on a T-shirt.

"It must be bloody hot in there," I said.

"Well, we've got exactly the same thing ahead of us, too," said Marianne. "Do you suppose they're infectious?"

"Why are they staring at us like that?" I asked.

There was a deathly hush. Only occasionally someone would cough. I lit a cigarette.

"Sometimes I think life would be more straightforward if you were ill," said Daniel. "Then you would know what to do, at least."

"Do you think the sick people believe in it?" asked Marianne.

"Sure," I said, "but it won't do them any good."

In the window immediately in front of us stood an old woman. Her arm hung down inertly. She was moving her fingers as though to test the material, or letting sand trickle through them. Behind us there was a noisy clatter. The metal shutters of the station café were being drawn up. A man in a white waistcoat brought a few plastic tables and chairs out onto the platform. When he disappeared back into the restaurant, I followed him.

"Water," Marianne called after me, and Daniel: "Me, too."

At the bar stood the stationmaster, who must have come in through the side entrance.

"A fatality," he said to me, and jerked his head in the direction of the white train, "and in this heat."

"It helped an aunt of mine," said the barman, "she had shingles. When she got back from Lourdes, it was gone. But the miracle wasn't confirmed. It made her so angry."

I ordered drinks for us.

"You're young," the stationmaster said to me. "I know when I was your age, I didn't use to think about things like that. A healthy constitution is the best present."

When I emerged from the café, Marianne said: "They're taking someone off the train."

"A fatality," I said. "I know. I heard."

The door of one car had been opened. Standing with his back to us was a man in a luminous orange waistcoat. His neck was glistening with sweat. He carefully backed down the steps, followed by a stretcher, followed by a second man in an orange waistcoat. The fat man in the dark suit and a nun brought up the rear. The sick people were now staring at the little group that had stopped next to the train. Then the nun ran along the train with little short steps, calling something, and flapping her hands, as though to shoo away chickens. A few of the sick people drew their heads in. Daniel laughed. The two ambulance men carried the stretcher away. The priest followed them.

"Can dead people sweat?" asked Daniel. "Or does all that stop right away?"

"They all knew it," said Marianne, "but they all kept staring at me anyway. Isn't that horrible?"

"I'm sure they must expect losses," said Daniel.

"It's horrible," said Marianne, "someone dies before our very eyes, and I go on rubbing cream into your back to stop you getting silly sunburn."

"He was dead when they got here," I said, "that's why they made a stop here. That's why they traveled so slowly."

"What does that have to do with it?" asked Marianne.

When the train moved off, the last of the sick people drew in their heads. The blinds came down.

"I'd like to know what time they'll get there," said Marianne. "How far do you think it is from here to Lourdes?"

"No idea," I said. "I can't imagine they'll be there before tomorrow morning."

"People are forever traveling," said Daniel, "even sick people. Even dead people. I'm sure they'll take him back to wherever he started out from. As if that made a difference."

I thought about the train rolling on through the night, going through towns and villages where people were asleep in their houses and didn't have a clue about those sick people who were unable to sleep because they were so excited, or in such pain. And how tomorrow morning, the Pyrenees would soar up out of the haze in front of them.

"A train full of sick people," I said, and Marianne shook her head.

DEEP FURROWS

D r. Kennedy appeared to be expecting an answer. He took a big swallow from his glass of beer, and looked at me. Birth, he had said, wasn't the opposite of death, it was the same thing.

"We come from death, and return to death. It's like entering a room and leaving it again."

Of course it was a commonplace, he said, everyone knew that the body was put together from chemicals, from inorganic matter, and would revert to it at the point of death. That's what they taught you at school, and then you forgot it, and started believing in some type of nonsense instead. I looked over at the musicians who were sitting and chatting in a ring in the middle of the pub. From time to time one or another of them would play one or two notes, sometimes one of the others would join in, but the melodies were invariably drowned out by the noise of the conversations. I had been given the name of the pub by Terry, whom I had met by chance on the street a couple of days previously. I was lost and asked him for directions, and he had accompanied me. We talked about music, and he recommended the community center to me. That was where they played real Irish music, he said, and everyone who had an instrument could play along. Sometimes he sang there himself. He painted as well, and wrote poems. He would give me a poem of his, if I came by there. When we parted he handed me his card, which read: Terry McAuley, genealogist. It was a laminated card, and once I'd read it, Terry put out his hand and I gave it back to him.

I had gotten to the center early, and had looked over the building. In one room there were a couple of guys facing each other, playing guitars, in another an old man was rehearsing a song with a group of children. The Gaelic text was up on a board on the wall, but the man spoke English with the children.

"As you sing, you ask the question, and give the answer," he said.

There were a few grown-ups sitting at the back of the room, listening. The doors to all the rooms were open, and the music mingled in the corridors. There was the sound of a bodhran from somewhere.

I went into the pub. The musicians came in one by one, a dozen men and women of all ages. They unpacked their instruments, fiddles and guitars, tin whistles and drums. A man tuned his fiddle, a woman played a couple of scales on a flute, the other musicians talked and laughed among themselves. Then Dr. Kennedy turned up and sat down opposite me, even though there were still some free tables.

I wanted to be quiet, but he immediately started talking to me. He introduced himself, and I told him my name. After that I didn't say a whole lot. With Dr. Kennedy, though, it was first one thing, then another.

Terry had come in, and sat down at the bar. I waved to him but he didn't react, it was as though he didn't see me. He ordered a pineapple juice. Did I know Terry, asked Dr. Kennedy. An unfortunate man, he said, an epileptic. He had used to work in the carpet factory, but had had so many fits that finally they'd had to let him go. Now he was unemployed, and living off the state.

"He used to be a good singer. Plus he was the best whistler in the region. He won competitions."

Then the doctor expressed his anger with Ireland and the Irish. It was incest, he said, that was to blame. That was what was at the root of the Troubles, unemployment, religious fanaticism, and alcoholism. That was why he himself had married a German woman. To import some fresh blood into the region. He had gone to Germany to look for a wife, a mother for his children. His wife was a Luther, and yes, some distant relation of the Reformation figure.

There was a short pause in the conversations all around. Dr. Kennedy was just saying he had three daughters, and in the sudden lull it sounded far too loud. A few of the guests laughed and looked across at us, and then everyone started talking together again.

The pub we were sitting in, the doctor went on to explain, had once been a fire station, then a community center in which only Gaelic was spoken. Nonsense, that was. Now it was open to everyone. Where did I come from? Switzerland was a beautiful country. There the peoples had mingled. Not like here.

Later on, Terry sang, and a few musicians accompanied him. But he wasn't a good singer, and eventually the musicians got bored, and ran away with the songs. Terry stumbled, and got tripped up on the words. Then the small audience clapped, till he put up his hands in modesty, and stopped singing.

I got myself a beer at the bar. When I came back, Dr. Kennedy asked me how long I planned on staying in Ireland. And why didn't I come and visit him. He often entertained visitors from abroad. Was I free tomorrow evening, for example. He gave me the address and stood up. I didn't get up.

The next evening, I went to Dr. Kennedy's house. It was on a hill at the edge of the city. I took a bus that drove through poor suburbs, and then out over green fields. The land on which the doctor's house was built was enclosed in a tall brick wall. On the wrought iron gate was a sign, *Deep Furrows*. I rang the bell. The gate opened with a low hum. As I walked through the garden to the house, the doctor came out to meet me. He shook my hand, and laid his arm on my shoulder, as if we were old friends.

"My wife and daughters are keenly anticipating your visit," he said, and led me to a slightly run-down white single-story house. Outside the door was a pond with goldfish in it. We walked into the house. Four women were standing in the corridor.

"My Cathy," said the doctor. "Kathleen. And my three daughters, Desiree, Emily, and Gwen." I shook hands four times. The doctor was talking about something or other, but I couldn't take my eyes off the three sisters. They closely resembled one another, they were all about thirty, all tall, all slender. Their faces were pale and serious, but ready to break out in spontaneous laughter. They all wore their hair long, Desiree's and Emily's was chestnut, Gwen's had a reddish tinge. All three wore skirts and old-fashioned blouses with lace trim, and thin woolen stockings. Dr. Kennedy asked me how I liked his daughters. I didn't know what to say. The sisters were very beautiful, but their beauty had something almost absurd because of the way it was repeated in all of them.

"Aren't they perfect creatures?" said the doctor, leading the way to the sitting room, where the table was already set.

Dr. Kennedy had told me in the pub that his wife would be glad for the chance to speak German again. But she barely said a word throughout the meal. She had greeted me in German, but with a strong English accent. I couldn't believe that she really was German. When I asked her where she'd grown up, she said it was somewhere in the east. She had lapsed back into English. While we ate, the doctor talked about politics and religion. He was a Protestant. I asked him if his name wasn't Irish. He shrugged his shoulders. His three daughters were as quiet as their mother, but they were very attentive. If I looked in their direction, they smiled and offered me wine, or passed me a dish if my plate was empty. Once I asked Gwen if it wasn't very isolated out here. She said they all loved the house. And there was plenty to do. Had I seen the garden?

"You can show our guest the garden tomorrow," said Dr. Kennedy.

The garden was Gwen's responsibility, he said. Desiree's was the accounts. She kept the books, and made sure there was always enough money in the house. And Emily? Emily was the most gifted of the three, and his favorite. She read a lot, and wrote, and played music and painted.

"She's our artist," said the doctor, and the women nodded and smiled. "Maybe she'll show you her portfolio tomorrow. But not tonight."

After supper, the sisters cleared the table, and Dr. Kennedy ushered me to his study. We sat down in leather chairs, and he poured whiskey and offered me a cigar. He talked some more about politics, and told me about his work in the hospital. He was an orthopedic surgeon, specializing in knee injuries. He told me about the way scores were settled in poor districts.

"If someone's caught with drugs, or stealing cars, or some kind of nonsense, he is told to appear at a certain time in a certain place, and they shoot him in the knee. If he doesn't appear at his summons, the whole family is expelled from the city."

It was stupid and pointless and disgusting, said the doctor. He shook his head, and poured more whiskey. From somewhere in the house, there was the sound of a violin. "Emily," said Dr. Kennedy, and he listened. A smile lit up his face.

Desiree came in. She went to the bookshelf, pulled down a book, and started leafing through it. The doctor inclined his head in her direction, and raised his eyebrows.

"You're very welcome," he said. "We'll all be extremely happy if you do."

Then he asked after my family, and where I had grown up. I looked across to Desiree. She smiled, lowered her gaze, and carried on leafing through her book. Was I often ill, the doctor wanted to know. I looked healthy, he could tell that from my eyes. Had my grandparents lived to a very great age? And were there any hereditary illnesses in the family, cases of insanity, for instance? I laughed.

"My profession," said the doctor in mitigation, and re-filled our glasses.

"As long as you don't want to take blood from me . . ."

"Why not?" he said smiling. "Why not, indeed."

I wasn't used to whiskey, and my head was spinning. When the doctor told me no buses ran at this time, and I was very welcome to stay the night, I didn't hang back and accepted his offer.

"Desiree will see to it that you're comfortable," he said, got up, and left. "Good night."

The music had stopped some while back. As I stepped out into the corridor with Desiree, I could hear the receding sound of the doctor's footsteps, and then everything was silent in the house. Desiree said they had all gone to bed. The days in *Deep Furrows* were filled with work, it was early to bed and early to rise. She took me to the guest bedroom, disappeared, and came back with a towel, a pair of pajamas, and a toothbrush. She said her room was next to mine. If I should want or need anything in the night, I was just to knock. She was a light sleeper.

I went to the bathroom. When I came back, Desiree was in my room. She had changed into a morning robe, and had pulled the comforter off the bed, and turned back the sheets. She was holding a glass of water. She asked if I wanted a hot water bottle, or if she should turn the heating higher, or draw the curtains? I thanked her, and said I had everything I needed. She set the water down on the nightstand, and remained standing next to the bed.

"I'll tuck you in," she said.

I had to laugh, and she laughed as well. But then I slipped into bed, and she tucked me in.

"If you were my brother," she said, "I would kiss you."

I woke up early. There was activity all over the house. I dropped off again. When I went into the kitchen it was past nine o'clock, and Gwen was just doing the dishes. She set the table for me, and said when I had finished breakfast she would show me the garden. Her father had gone into town with her mother, and Desiree was in the office. As I ate, I heard the violin again, a sad, quiet tune.

"Isn't it beautiful?" Gwen said. "The music, the house, everything?"

"You should be here in springtime," she said as she led me through the garden. She showed me the hydrangeas, the lilac and hibiscus bushes she was especially proud of. She talked about her successes with breeding and grafting plants, and various prizes she'd won. She had a pair of clippers in her hand and as she spoke, she would sometimes stoop to chop at a slug, and watch as the body writhed around its frothing wound. That was how she pictured Paradise to herself, a garden of God, and the blessed who planted and tended it.

"A life with flowers and for flowers," she said, "to be always in the garden, in summer and winter alike. And to be working there."

When I'd arrived there the night before, a stormy wind had been blowing, but here in the garden the air was still and calm. The sky was gray, the light a little dim, as though it had been filtered on its way down to us.

Gwen took me by the hand, and said she wanted to show me something. She led me to a little stand of trees at the edge of the property. Under an oak tree with oddly shaped, waxy leaves, there was an old stone slab in the ground. "My grandparents," she said. "They were born here, and they died here. Both on the same day." Gwen knelt down, and brushed the stone with her hands.

When you're in the grave, my love,
In the darkness of the tomb,
I'll climb down to you from above,
And press myself against you.

Gwen said the poem out loud in German. At first it failed to register. I asked her to say it again.

"Our mother taught us poems," she said. "It's so beautiful. So much pain, and so much desire." Her grandparents had died on the same day, she said again, that was how much they had loved each other. The funeral had been a joyful occasion. I knelt down to try and decipher the writing on the stone. I could only just manage to read the names, the year of birth was wiped away, the year of death was 1880-something.

"How can they have been your grandparents, if they died over a hundred years ago?" I asked. "And how can you remember the funeral?"

But Gwen had disappeared. I heard a rustling in the leaves, and stood up, and walked into the stand of trees. Gwen was ahead of me, sometimes I could see her form in among the trees. When I caught up with her, she stood leaning against the high wall that surrounded the property. She said: "I am the lily of the valley, and you the apple tree."

She laughed and looked straight at me, until I lowered my eyes. Then she pushed off the wall, and set off for the house. Her hands were folded behind her back. I followed her at a short distance. When she reached the rose beds, she told me to go on inside, she had something she needed to see to.

Inside the house, it was quiet. Only the soft tone of the violin, always playing the same run of notes. I went to the kitchen, and poured a cup of coffee. The music had stopped, and then it began again. It was a familiar tune, but I don't know where I had heard it before. I went looking for it, and came to a door. The music sounded very near now. When I knocked, it stopped, there was silence for a moment, and then the door opened.

"I was waiting for you," said Emily, and she told me to come in.

"What was that tune you were playing?"

"Oh, I was just playing," she said, "it's something I made up."

She pointed me to the sofa with her bow. I sat down, and Emily started playing again. Her expression was concentrated, almost worried. The music was very beautiful. The melodies seemed to merge into one another, and I often had the sense of recognizing one or another of them, but then I couldn't think where from. Suddenly Emily broke off in the middle of a tune. She said she couldn't find the ending, she just had to go on and on playing. The only reason she played was to find the ending. She even dreamed of finding it, sometimes.

"I'm walking in the garden. I hear the tune, it doesn't stop. I know the tune, but not the resolution. I'm looking for it in the garden. Then my father finds me. He takes my coat away. And when I wake up, I can't find it anywhere."

Emily sat down beside me on the sofa. She leaned over her violin, which she held cradled in her arms like a child. Her head was to one side, as if she were trying to listen to some distant sound. I asked her whether she hadn't ever thought of leaving here. She slowly shook her head and said: "I have already taken off my dress, how can I possibly put it on again?"

She put her violin away with a gesture of impatience, and said: "Anyway, where would we go?"

I asked her whether she would show me her paintings. She shook her head.

"When you come back," she said.

I said I was going now.

"I won't see you out," she said, and got up with me. I thought she wanted to kiss me on the cheek, but instead she whispered something in my ear, and pushed me out the door. As I walked through the house, I heard Emily begin to play again, the same sad melody she had played last night and this morning, and that I still couldn't identify.

I left the house, and walked through the garden. Gwen was nowhere to be seen. The gate was locked. I scrambled over the wall, and was relieved to be standing out on the street. I didn't want to wait for a bus, and set off down the hill. Earlier on, the sky had been overcast, now a fresh wind was blowing an ever darkening succession of clouds across the sky. The trees beside the road were moving violently, as though trying to tear loose from the earth. In the east, it looked like rain. I had almost reached the foot of the hill, when an old white Mercedes approached. It drew up alongside me. Dr. Kennedy leaned across the front passenger seat, and wound down the window.

"Are you going already?" he asked. "Who let you out?"

He said I could perfectly well stay as long as I liked. I said I didn't have anything with me, all my things were back at the B and B. He said he would drive me there, we could pick up my things, and be back here in no time. He opened the door, and I got in.

On the way into town, it started raining. I asked Dr. Kennedy about the grave in his garden. He said he didn't know who was buried there. He had bought the property thirty years ago. They had come across the stone in the course of building work. He said the dead were of no interest to him. Then he asked me which of his daughters I liked best. I said they were all three beautiful.

"Yes, they're beautiful all right," he said, "but now you have to make up your mind. We will all be very happy."

We drove through an area of ugly tenement blocks. Children were playing by the roadside, and a couple of men standing with cans of beer outside a fish truck turned to stare at us. I asked the doctor whether this was a Catholic or Protestant part of town. That didn't matter, he said, misery was the same everywhere. Like happiness, indeed. He said he found it all repulsive. I asked him whether he had never considered moving away. He said he had built a wall around his house. And he took note of who came into his garden. He asked me who had let me out, and looked at me.

"I climbed over the wall," I said.

The doctor's face became expressionless. He looked tired. He didn't say anything, and watched the road again. He stopped outside the B and B and said he would wait for me in the car.

I went to my room, and packed my things. I thought of all that I had seen and all that I might yet see. I looked out the window. The white Mercedes was parked outside. The rain had stopped, and the doctor had gotten out, and was pacing back and forth on the pavement. He was smoking a cigarette and seemed nervous.

I had packed everything, but I didn't go downstairs. I stayed by the window, looking down. The doctor walked back and forth. He dropped a butt in the gutter, and lit himself another cigarette. Once, he looked up at me, but he couldn't have seen me through the curtains. He waited probably half an hour, then he got into the old Mercedes and drove off.

I thought of the evening I had first met Dr. Kennedy. After he had gone, I sat on at my table. I drank my beer, and waited, I don't know what for. Then a tune surfaced through the noise. One of the musicians had begun to play, and gradually the others fell in. The conversations at the tables grew quieter, and finally stopped altogether.

The music was at once sad and cheerful, melancholy and rousing and full of strength. It filled the room, and didn't stop. The younger players, children some of them, gradually packed away their instruments and went away, but the rest carried on playing, and others came along and filled in the gaps in the circle. When the drummer left, he handed Terry his drum, and now Terry was playing along with them too, hesitantly at first, then with a growing confidence. Among the musicians I remembered the old man who had coached the children in their singing the day before. He was playing the fiddle. He looked very serious.

I stood by the window of the pension, and looked out. The clouds passed swiftly across the sky, continually changing their shape. They were moving from east to west, crossing the island, and moving out to the Atlantic. I stood there for a long time, thinking about the music and the old man and what he had said to the children. You have to ask the question, and give the answer. It's one and the same thing.

THE EXPERIMENT

I met Chris on a basketball court, way uptown in Manhattan. Guys from the neighborhood met up to play there, and you could turn up when you liked, and play till you were tired. Chris was the only white guy I ever saw there. Whenever he was playing he wanted proper teams, and he kept score, and he objected when someone held the ball too long.

When I got tired, I would sit in the shade of some trees at the edge of the court, and watch the others. One time, Chris sat down alongside me, and asked if I lived locally. We talked for a while and got along pretty well, and when I told him I was looking for a room he suggested I move in with him. He had just split up with his girlfriend, he said, and was looking for a subtenant.

We shared the apartment for a little while, without seeing much of one another. Then Chris fell in love at a college party. He told me all about it that same night. I had already been asleep. It was past midnight when he woke me.

"I've fallen in love," he said.

"That's nice for you," I said, "now can I go back to sleeping, please."

"She's an Indian girl called Yotslana. She had the most amazing jet-black hair you can imagine. And her eyes . . ."

The following evening, we talked about women and love. Chris was raving about his Yotslana, and maybe because it was getting on my nerves, I argued that true love could never be physical. The physical corrupted everything, it opened your eyes, and destroyed any ideal, spiritual love.

"I think you should keep your one great love unconsummated," I said. "It doesn't matter if you have other relationships on the side, it doesn't even matter if you live with another woman."

Chris listened silently. For the next few weeks, he was thoughtful. He stopped talking about Yotslana. He met her from time to time, and after those meetings he would get home late. When fall came around, I moved to Chicago. Chris helped me pack my things, and drove me to the station.

"How's your Indian girl?" I asked.

"We're in love. She's moving in. She's quarreled with her parents, and of course your room's vacant."

"Good luck," I said, and promised to visit in the spring.

In Chicago, I found myself living with a young couple in a big apartment on the South Side. She was a dancer, he was a photographer. He was Brazilian, and the two of them had married so that he could remain in the country. He was gay, the dancer explained my first evening there, but they were very devoted to each other, maybe more than most couples, because they didn't expect anything of one another. Sometimes he would come to her bed on Sunday mornings, and then he would be like a child.

The winter was very cold, but our apartment was cozy and light. Nelson, the photographer's boyfriend, came around most nights, and when the two of them disappeared into the bedroom the dancer laughed, and turned the music louder. Each of us lived his or her own life, but we would have the occasional communal meal together, and listen to piano music by Chopin and Ravel. And sometimes, three or four of us would lie side by side in the big bed, watching old episodes of *Star Trek* on television.

In the spring I went to New York for two weeks. I had called Chris. He had said I could come and stay with them, with him and Yotslana.

I turned up in the evening, Chris opened the door. "Shame," he said, "Yotslana's staying with a friend. But you'll get to meet her tomorrow."

We cooked dinner, and reminisced about last summer, and I talked about my time in Chicago, and my roommates, and the icy wind in the windy city. Chris seemed impatient to tell me something. As we were washing up, he said quite abruptly: "You know, Yotslana and me . . . we're not sleeping together."

I didn't know what to say. Chris took a couple of beers out of the fridge, and we sat down in the living room. The only light was the little desk lamp. There were piles of books all over the room.

"We're in love," he said. "I've never loved a woman so much. But we don't sleep together."

"But you're almost on top of each other in this place . . ."

Chris stood up, and strode quickly to the bookcase that was almost in the dark. He turned around to me.

"We sleep in the same bed," he said, and laughed. "It's killing me. We don't touch. It's an experiment."

Neither of us said anything. When Chris resumed, I couldn't see his face at all clearly.

"I got the idea from something you said. It's the only way of saving love from banality and habit."

"That was just for the sake of argument. I never believed in it. My God! It's madness."

"Well," said Chris, "it works. We love each other as much as on the first day."

The following morning, I met Yotslana. She must have come into the house while I was asleep. She had taken a shower, and was wearing a short bathrobe, and she was every bit as beautiful as Chris had described. She sat at the kitchen table, reading a book. I introduced myself.

"Chris is at school already," said Yotslana. "Do you want coffee?"

I sat down opposite her. She didn't say much, but looked at me searchingly. We drank the coffee.

Then Yotslana went into the bedroom, and I left the apartment and headed downtown.

I got along well with Yotslana. She didn't often have to go to school, and on some days we went for walks in the park, and talked about all kinds of things. Sometimes she would link arms with me, and we would talk about Chris, things about him that bothered her. That he was so stubborn and pedantic, the way he took everything so seriously.

"He's a theorist," she said, "a cerebral type. I'm the opposite. I'm a gut person."

When I was shaving on one of the following mornings, Yotslana walked into the bathroom. She started undressing behind my back. I could see her in the mirror, I could see her back, her wide shoulders, her slender neck as she pinned back her hair. She turned around. Our eyes met in the mirror, and Yotslana smiled and got into the old bathtub to shower. I hurriedly finished shaving, but already she was peeping around the edge of the shower curtain, saying: "Will you pass me the towel, please."

She took the towel from me, got out of the tub, and dried herself.

"India must be a very beautiful country," I said.

She laughed, and took the big bottle of baby lotion off the windowsill, and started putting it on all over herself.

I had gone over to the door, but Yotslana never stopped engaging me in conversation. I looked at my hands, at the ceiling, in every conceivable direction. Then Yotslana threw me the damp towel. She stopped talking, and I sat down on the toilet seat and watched her. She lotioned her arms, her breasts, her belly, her thighs. She perched on the edge of the tub, and carefully applied lotion to her feet, toe by toe.

"Will you rub my back, please?" she asked, stepped up to me, pushed the bottle into my hands, and turned around.

I stood up. I rubbed her neck, her shoulders, her back, her lower back. I stroked her waist, her hips, her bottom, all the while trying to keep my eyes on my hands rather than her body. Yotslana turned around, and my hands continued to move, slid over her body, followed and then directed by her hands. Then there was only one hand. Yotslana had directed it, and left it to its own devices. She was propping herself against the washbasin, and she had her eyes shut.

When the soap dish slid onto the ground and shattered, Yotslana laughed and laid her hands on mine, picked it up, and kissed my fingertips.

"You smell of me."

"If Chris comes back . . ."

"You might have thought of that earlier."

Later we showered together, and I dried Yotslana with the towel that was still wet.

"Shall we eat something together?" I asked.

"No time," she said. "I've got to be somewhere at twelve."

In the afternoon I went over to the basketball court, but there was no one there. It had rained a lot in the last few days, and the asphalt court was covered with leaves from the past fall. I didn't get back to the apartment till after dark. Chris was cooking. He asked me if I wanted to eat with him.

"Yotslana's staying the night with a friend," he said. "How do you like her?"

"She's very beautiful," I said. I was ashamed of myself.

We put away a lot of beer that night. Just like old times, said Chris.

"Are you okay, you and Yotslana? Isn't it inevitable that one day one or the other of you will . . ."

Chris shrugged his shoulders.

A few days later, I got back from the city earlier than usual. I had been out since morning. It was raining, and as the rain got heavier about lunchtime, I decided to go home. Yotslana wasn't there. I heard voices and laughter from the bedroom. I went to the kitchen to fix some coffee. Then Chris wandered in with a woman. He was wearing just a pair of jeans, she was in a long T-shirt. The three of us drank coffee. Then the woman got dressed and left. Chris told me not to say anything about it to Yotslana.

"She knows Meg from school."

"Meg?" I asked.

"She's not my type, but she's quite sweet. Yotslana can't bear her."

I felt relieved.

Yotslana was behaving strangely in those days. If Chris was there, she would exchange loving looks with him, but the second he was gone she would come to me, and throw her arms around me, and let me embrace her.

It had rained again, all afternoon, and we lay together on my bed. I lay on my back, Yotslana on her belly. We were splitting a can of beer. I touched Yotslana's naked shoulder blades with the ice-cold can, and ran it down her spine. She turned over, took the can out of my hand, and set it down on her belly.

"Could you imagine living in Chicago?" I asked.

"No," she said, "Chicago's way too cold."

"New York's cold too."

"Anyway this is where I'm studying."

"I could come back to New York . . ."

"No," said Yotslana crossly. She pressed the can into my hand, got up, and walked to the bathroom.

"I love you," I called out after her. I felt ridiculous.

Yotslana didn't reply. I heard her in the shower, and later on she left the apartment.

On my last evening in the city I cooked for Chris and Yotslana. We were drinking coffee when I said: "I love Yotslana."

Chris looked at me with a smile.

Yotslana said: "You're crazy."

"We've slept together," I went on, without paying her any attention. Chris sighed and shrugged his shoulders. Yotslana tried to take his hand. Then she crossed her arms and leaned way back in her chair.

"The soap dish," said Chris, and shook his head.

"Also, Chris and Meg . . ." I said.

"Meg?" said Yotslana, and twisted her face in a scornful smile.

Chris held up his hands in embarrassment, and dropped them again.

"My God," he said. "I'm only human."

"What's the matter with you two," I said. I was furious. "I love Yotslana!"

Yotslana sipped her coffee and said: "Two bodies collide with each other and separate from one another."

"That was your idea," said Chris. "That you shouldn't sleep with the woman you truly love. We thought about it a long time. And it works. Only everyone keeps falling in love with Yotslana."

"If I go to bed with a man, he thinks it means I want to marry him," she said. "It's easier for Chris. Women aren't so emotional."

I wasn't listening, and just repeated: "Yotslana, I love you!"

She laid her hand on my arm.

"I like you," she said. "You're different from Chris. So romantic."

"Yotslana fell in love with you a little bit," said Chris. "So I told her she should sleep with you. To put a stop to it."

THE KISS

She had suggested to her father that she collect him in Basel. That's all I need, he had said. He wasn't some kid, traveling on his own for the first time. She couldn't remember that he had ever gone anywhere on his own. She had noted the times of the train arrivals at the station, and had sent her father an itinerary: change in Frankfurt and Basel. You get here at 12:48. If I'm not there, wait for me in the station restaurant. I won't be long.

Take a roomette. The way she said that. She traveled all the way to Switzerland with up to five others in a compartment. But that wasn't appropriate for an old man, and least of all, someone like him. She hadn't said that. She had said: Give yourself a treat, for once. On the rare occasion you do come and see me. You can share my room, that way you'll save on the hotel.

He hadn't slept in the same room as her since she was a baby. Then, they had only had three rooms and a gas stove. At night, Mette had gotten up and fed the baby, and he had pretended to be asleep. How could you call a child Inger? As she got older, he became used to it. But that tiny scrap of a thing going by Inger. He had had a hundred names for her, only Inger was never one of them.

If she hadn't occasionally visited home, they would never have seen each other at all. She drove home for her mother's funeral, and after Christmas, when the owner shut the restaurant for two weeks so that she could go and vacation in Egypt. Why didn't he ever visit her? She had had to ask him: please come. You've got enough time now. But didn't she like coming home, he said. I go on your account. And she waited for him to say: You don't have to come on my account. He had already opened his mouth, but he didn't say anything.

He had never gone anywhere on his own. He had married young, before that he had never been able to afford to travel, and much less afterwards. At that time, they stayed put. Later on, they vacationed, in Italy or Spain, as a family. When the children were grown up, they didn't feel like it anymore, and he and Mette traveled by themselves. They took a cruise down the Danube, and once they visited the Christmas fair at Nuremberg. Since Mette's death, he hadn't been anywhere.

Even the station was an adventure to him then. The night train from Copenhagen made only a short stop. He was the only passenger who got on. The conductor asked him what his destination was. He only let him board the train once he'd seen his ticket. After that, he was suddenly very friendly. When would you like me to wake you? Would you like anything else? Coffee? Beer? A sandwich? He wasn't hungry. He had got to the station far too early, and had eaten a hot dog. He was nervous. He went along to the dining car. The conductor locked the compartment with a special key.

Even by the time of her third trip, Inger knew how everything worked. She took one of the top bunks. It was warmer up there than below, and you felt protected. She shared the compartment with a couple of young men who were on their way to a soccer game, and with a woman in practical-looking clothes. The three had been on the train since Copenhagen. The men stood out in the corridor and drank beer and smoked, she only got to meet the woman the following morning. She could have been her mother.

He drank a beer, and then another. There was a group of young people at one of the other tables. They were going to a fair in Frankfurt, and they were in good spirits. He thought of his suitcase, in the locked compartment. He had brought a can of herrings in curry sauce with him, and a pack of salted licorice. He knew what Inger liked. When she left home, Mette had already been sick. Mama isn't well, that was all he had said. And Inger hadn't said anything, and had left.

Mama wasn't well. As if that was a reason to stay home. It was a reason to go. He always spoke of her as Mama when he was talking to Inger. Go and apologize to Mama. Mama's not well. Mama's sick. Sometimes, Inger had wanted just to call her Mette, as her father did. Even the cousins called her by her name. But then she hadn't done it. She didn't want any dissension. When her mother died, everything changed. Only he failed to notice.

He swayed through the narrow corridors of the train. Was his compartment in the third car along, or the fourth? The way back is always shorter, he had often told Inger when they went for walks on Sundays. The way back was always shorter. But Inger didn't want to go back. Inger wanted to go on.

Every day she saw the trains, heard the trains, that were going south into the big tunnel. She would find a job in Italy. She didn't ask for much. A room and whatever the going wage was. She wanted to have fun, meet people who didn't know anything about her except what she told them. And she wouldn't tell them anything. She didn't want to think about Odense, about home and family. The way they sat there chewing over old times, and telling the same stories over and over again. She wanted to go on, and not back. Everyone comes back some time, her father had said. And asked her what he ought to bring. Nothing. You can get everything here. How about licorice? If you like. Herrings? She didn't say anything. Whatever you like, she said, and thought if I miss anything, it's licorice. But she didn't want any arguments. As long as there were arguments, you were dependent on someone. You only got to be independent when you no longer asked for anything. Not even to be left in peace. Whatever you like, she had said. She had said: take some heavy shoes. We'll be going hiking.

That was something he had always said: We're going hiking. Inger didn't want to go. She wanted to watch TV, sit at home, waste away her Sundays. The exercise will do you good. You can sit all day at school. Sometimes he envied her for feeling happy in the house. He had never liked being at home, and even then he had never left.

At 12:48 she was still in the restaurant. From noon, she had looked at her watch every couple of minutes. Don't you need to go, asked the hostess. It wasn't more than five minutes to the station, but the trains ran on time here. In a minute, she said. She was sure he wouldn't go to the station restaurant. He would wait for her on the platform, not even sit on a bench. He would stand next to his suitcase and make some remark about her unpunctuality. It wouldn't even occur to him that she had come late on purpose. Perhaps she was looking for an argument, after all.

He stood next to his suitcase. He had a book with him. He could have sat down to read, but he was annoyed about her unpunctuality. He wanted to be annoyed. He was always annoyed when he got excited about something. They hadn't seen each other for three months.

In the context of three months, what are ten minutes? Twelve minutes. She hugged him. Ever since the funeral, it was hugs all round. It had just happened like that. She liked to be touched. The hostess's hand around her waist, just casually, when they happened to be standing behind the bar together. The hands of men, brushing hers, when she stepped up to the tables. And when she touched herself. But hugging her father. That didn't feel right. She felt sorry for him, and that was disagreeable to her.

So this is where you live? It was a question he had prepared on his way down, and also the reproachful tone of it. The real question was: Why don't you come home? The valley was dark, the village was ugly, and the noise from the cars was never-ending. He was surprised to find all his prejudices confirmed. He didn't ask his question. It was too abundantly clear that she couldn't live there. The place was a hollow, a funnel feeding into the tunnel. Seventeen kilometers, said Inger, there's a different climate on the other side, a different language, a different world. Over there is the south, here is the north. You can also go over the pass. The train had passed through many tunnels on its way. The mouths of all the tunnels were the same. You only got to learn how long they were when you came out the other side.

He greeted the owner politely, he made a good impression, he did at least owe Inger that much. A real gentleman. How old was he? And what was his job? And such good German too. He's retired, said Inger.

She had shown him up to the room, and then she'd gone back down to the restaurant. If you like—but she knew he wouldn't show his face down here. Even so, she looked at the door every time someone came in. He would stay up in the room till she came to get him at the end of her shift. She thought about him all afternoon. When she got off at six, it was already dark outside. She slowly climbed the steps. There was no hurry. He suddenly seemed ridiculous to her, sitting up there alone in the tiny dark room, waiting. The owner would have let her go a little earlier. But Inger didn't want to go. He was to learn that she had a job, had her own life, that she hadn't waited for him.

He had been waiting for her. He was standing in the middle of the room as if he hadn't moved from the spot all afternoon. He had been preparing himself. His daughter seeing fit to work in such a place. Waiting tables. When she had a degree, and a profession. If it's just a question of money. It suits me this way. But it doesn't suit me. The whole village seemed to be like a dark, cramped little room to him. When are you coming home? I'm not. How do I know.

We could go to the Ticino, she said, in the south. What for? Because it's beautiful there. Is that a good enough reason? She didn't know. She had never been there on her own. She took off her blouse and her black skirt, and washed in the basin. Did she resemble her mother? He had hardly any photos from her early years. You've got a tattoo? So he was watching her. No. She laughed and stepped closer to him. You can wash it off. Well, then wash it off. Childish nonsense. What have you got it for? A rose. From the station kiosk. She had bought some candy. They didn't have salty licorice here, but they had other things. Shall we get something to eat? What do you feel like eating? He didn't mind. He asked if they cooked properly here at least. Yes, they do, she said. But we'll go out for supper. Tomorrow we'll go walking, okay? Hiking.

She had set up a camp bed in the room. She would sleep there for the time her father stayed. She didn't sleep well. She heard him breathing loudly, and tossing and turning. When she got up to go to the bathroom, she passed by the bed. Sleeping, he looked older than he did awake. She didn't see him as her father, she saw him as an old man, the withered body of an old man who was utterly strange to her. She couldn't imagine anything connecting her and this old man.

He had woken up two hours before her, had been sitting at the table reading. She had woken up when he got up, but she had pretended to be still asleep. On the days when she did the early shift, she had to get up at half past five. She opened the restaurant at half past six. The driver of the bus would be standing outside already, who always went to Denmark for his vacation, and knew one or two words of Danish. *Good morning, how are you, my name is Alois, I love you.* He laughed, and she laughed, and corrected his accent. *I love you, I love you, I love you.* Again and again, till it sounded right. Then he read the newspaper, and she set out the ashtrays on the tables.

Her father stood beside the camp bed. It's my day off, she said, and turned over. And then she got up after all. We could catch a bus or train somewhere. But he wanted to hike. It had stopped raining. What if it started again? That wouldn't bother him.

She told him the story of the Devil's Bridge. He didn't

say anything. He breathed heavily. The path was narrow and steep, and he walked unsteadily. When she wanted to rest, he drove them on. Only then did she notice that he was frightened.

They walked across a steep slope. To him it felt as though the earth had turned over, and everything was skewed and unsafe. There was nowhere to orient yourself, and no holds. The moraine slipped away under your feet. It was an easy path, she said. Even for a Dane. What have you got against Denmark? He was annoyed. Those people who emigrated and badmouthed their native country. Do you want to live here then? In this hole? She shook her head. You don't have to be so aggressive.

She walked on. Her father followed her in silence. It was almost noon, but it had grown hardly any lighter in this narrow valley. There was a Russian bus by the Devil's Bridge. We can do the last bit on the road. Why? Well, if you're having trouble with the scree . . . It was no trouble. You never find anything difficult, ha? You can do any-thing. You know everything. You never make any mis-takes. Of course he made mistakes. For instance? Coming here was a mistake, for one. If you want to leave . . . He didn't reply. He walked behind her, along the road, even though there was hardly any traffic.

She didn't want to quarrel. She wanted to be with her father the way she had been with him when she was a child. He was besotted with her, her mother had often said so. But only when he wasn't listening. If she opened her mouth, it was all over. He had stopped. When she turned around and saw him standing by the side of the road, she knew she was stronger than he was.

That night she stood beside his bed again. Then she lay down next to him, carefully, so as not to wake him. In his sleep he turned toward her. He placed a hand on her hip. She lay perfectly still beside him, he was sleeping more calmly now. Later on, she moved back to the camp bed again. In the morning she asked him if he'd dreamed anything. He said he never dreamed. She said everyone dreamed.

The weather was better. What shall we do today? We could take the train a ways, and then walk ... But he wanted to walk up the valley again. Why? It's where we were yesterday. Why not? This time he went ahead. He seemed to feel more confident now. Sometimes they saw the railway line on their climb, and once the path crossed over the road on a viaduct. You could step right up to the edge and look down.

Inger! he called, not so close to the edge. He had never been to the mountains before, he had no idea about mountains. On the pictures he knew, they were always in the distance, a feature of the horizon, small seeming. The Alps were formed when Europe and Africa collided. You don't have to tell me about the Alps. You will never belong here. What if I meet a man here, and marry him? It's your life. Is it? He reflected. Do you have any friends here? Do you have a boyfriend? Why not?

Why not? She thought about it. She didn't want a boyfriend. Casual touches were enough for her. She didn't want to stay here. If it wasn't for the tunnel, she would have run off long ago. Every hour there was a train south. One day she would get on one of them. If you like, she said, we can go to the Ticino tomorrow.

They had almost reached their destination, and were walking side by side on a bicycle track. He was telling her something. When you were little you fixed a piece of cardboard to your bike with a clothespin, so that it got in the spokes. It rattled like a motorbike. You were so proud, and you couldn't stop. I punished you. Afterwards, I felt sorry. She couldn't remember. It wasn't just that time either. Do you think I was difficult? You were a child. What do you mean? He didn't reply, and really she didn't want to know what he meant by it. It was enough for her to have him walking along beside her.

He had made the same mistakes as his own father. A bit late to think of that now. Everyone made mistakes. There was no point talking about it, thinking about it. She had forgotten, and he should forget about it too. He didn't know what made him think about it now.

If you're not too tired? They walked beyond where they had got to the day before. The gradient leveled out, and the path led across a meadow. They had almost reached the next village when it started to rain. There was a remote gas station on the road. They sheltered there. The weather is very changeable here, said Inger. Sometimes it snows in summer. Aren't you cold? A VW van stopped at the gas station. A man got out. There were three children in the back seat. One of them wiped the condensation off the window. He stared at Inger. Then he poked his tongue at her. The man finished filling up. He climbed in, and drove off.

Inger hadn't been popular as a child, she had never found out why. She had tried to make friends, but she had never had very many. You made a fuss of yourself, said her father. You always wanted to be the center of attention. Sometimes it would drive me crazy. Inger had always seen herself as a victim. It's a good thing to be grown-up, she said. Because you get left in peace. Because you don't owe anyone anything. Tell me about Mama. What was she like when you married. Ah, he said.

The driver of the bus had seen Inger on the road, and stopped. Do you want a ride? This is my father. This is Alois. They drove up to the pass. The bus stopped there for twenty minutes, and Alois tried out his repertoire of sentences on Inger and her father. He said: *Good morning, how are you, my name is Alois. I would like a cup of coffee.* And then, in his own language: *Can I take you on to Airolo?* Inger shook her head. Some other time. Maybe tomorrow.

She took her father by the hand, and they ran through the rain to the inn. It was cold up here, and he was in his shirt. Aren't you cold? Come on, we'll make some tea. On the way back, he was coughing. He didn't want to take her jacket, she simply laid it over his shoulders. For a moment she left her arm there.

In the evening he had a temperature. When she moved to put her palm on his forehead, he turned his head away. It's nothing. They ate downstairs, in the restaurant. He wasn't hungry, and when he climbed the stairs in front of her, he staggered as though drunk. Now he was asleep, and she was sitting at the table, reading a magazine he had brought her. She imagined: He's the child, and I'm the mother. He's sick. She went up to the bed, laid her hand on his brow. He seemed helpless. But what could she do? She imagined: If he gets sick at home, there's no one there to look after him. She saw him traipse through the house in his pajamas. He was sick in the bathroom, he cleaned himself up, he went to the kitchen and made tea. He didn't turn on the light, he knew where everything was kept. Inger switched off the light on the nightstand, and got into bed with him. She lay there still for a long time, and then she kissed him on the mouth. At that moment, she was prepared to forgive him for everything.

When he woke up, she had gone to sleep. He wasn't surprised to find her next to him in bed. He took her hand, which lay on the sheet. In the sparse light, he could only just dimly make out her face. He looked at her for a long time. She resembled her mother. But that was so long ago. Perhaps he was just imagining it, perhaps he was dreaming. When he awoke again, it was morning. Inger stood in front of the sink. He was glad she wasn't lying beside him.

He wouldn't have known what to say. Inger? he said. She turned to face him. Do you feel better? Yes, he said, and smiled. If you like, we can go south today.

He was talking more softly than usual, she could hardly hear him. As she washed, she could hear him getting up. He went up to the window and opened it. Cool air came in. She didn't know what it was that made her think about his death, now, for the very first time.

Printed in the United States
by Baker & Taylor Publisher Services